**Of all the crazy moves Vonya had pulled,
nothing compared to the insanity of standing
in the dark corridor outside Tyn Cathedral**

How she wished Brody were standing here with her—if not holding her hand, at least close enough to hear her scream should someone jump out of the shadows.

She startled at a young man who looked about eighteen.

"Did Bishop send you?"

"Whatya have?"

She dug into her pocket, pulled out the computer.

A crack shocked the air, and she jumped back.

The kid collapsed, his body lying with eyes wide in the dim glow of a jewelry store's display.

She stood there, unable to move or breathe.

A second shot shattered the glass window beside her.

Her legs moved then, fast. She ducked down a road, turned into another alley and sprinted.

An arm snaked around her, clamping over her mouth. "I found you."

She slammed a fist into her captor's leg, landing her foot on his instep. He woofed out a breath, let her go and she whirled.

"Ronie!" he said.

She gulped a breath. "Brody!" She launched herself into his arms.

And then, because that's what he did, he lifted her and carried her away.

Books by Susan May Warren

Love Inspired Suspense

*Point of No Return
*Mission: Out of Control

*Missions of Mercy

Steeple Hill

*In Sheep's Clothing
Everything's Coming Up Josey
Sands of Time
Chill Out, Josey!
Wiser Than Serpents
Get Cozy, Josey!*

SUSAN MAY WARREN

is a RITA® Award-winning, bestselling novelist of more than twenty-five novels. She has won an Inspirational Readers Choice Award, an ACFW Book of the Year award and has been a Christy Award finalist. Her compelling plots and unforgettable characters have won her acclaim with readers and reviewers alike. She and her husband of twenty years and their four children live in a small town on Minnesota's beautiful Lake Superior shore, where they are active in their local church. You can find her online at www.susanmaywarren.com.

MISSION: OUT OF CONTROL

SUSAN MAY WARREN

Steeple
Hill®

Published by Steeple Hill Books™

STEEPLE HILL BOOKS

Steeple
Hill®

Recycling programs
for this product may
not exist in your area.

ISBN-13: 978-0-373-44432-8

MISSION: OUT OF CONTROL

www.SteepleHill.com

Printed in U.S.A.

And God demonstrates his own love for us in this:
while we were yet sinners, Christ died for us.
—*Romans* 5:8

To Andrew, David, Sarah, Peter and Noah,
and my secret weapons Rachel Hauck, Ellen Tarver
for helping me craft a book that
I pray brings glory to the Lord.

ONE

Was it too much to ask for a little peace and quiet on his so-called R & R?

Apparently Brody Wickham—ex-Green Beret, current on-leave security operator for Stryker International—had turned into a magnet for trouble, and he knew inside his gut that someone was going to get hurt.

Preferably not him.

Brody could spot the ugly future the second that Vonya—the one-name, brazen rock 'n' roll diva and the leader of the crazies inside this D.C. nightclub—stepped up to the edge of the stage and, with a feral scream, sprang into the outstretched hands of her minions.

Perhaps *soared* might be a better term, as she launched herself, arms flung out, like some sort of prehistoric animal in scaly black leather and a peacock mask, her garish pink wig a plume, into the undulating mosh pit.

Thankfully, anonymous hands caught Miss Crazy and floated her over the mass like a piece of bacon. It didn't mean this wouldn't end badly. With blood. Broken bones.

Death by stampede.

And Brody Wickham, off-duty bodyguard, simply

couldn't let that happen, despite wanting to stay incognito in the shadows near the bar. He moved to the edge of the crowd, every muscle coiled. He'd guess that in about ten seconds, he'd have to plow through this mob and save her.

He should be sitting on a lawn chair in the backyard of his parents' suburban ranch home, catching up on the news of his eight brothers and sisters—most of whom he hadn't seen for nearly a decade. Or helping his parents decipher the foreclosure notice from the bank.

The music nearly shook the bricks from their mortar in the warehouse-turned-club, the perfect venue for Vonya's eccentric pulse, with its black Art Deco walls covered in skinny mirrors, disco lights dangling from the ceiling, and a round stage that thrust out into the audience.

Despite the cacophony of noise, he had to admit, Vonya had pipes. Brody wasn't so iron-eared as to not recognize the flash of talent in the tones that blew out of that petite body covered in leather and fishnet, even if he spent most of the night averting his eyes from her plunging minidress.

A random elbow connected with the soft tissue of his nose, stopping him cold at the fringes of the dancers.

Okay, what was he *doing?* This wasn't his gig, his battle. He didn't even know this impulsive woman, and nobody had asked him to be a hero today.

He was here for—

Lucy! She'd jumped right into the mosh pit, moving to the middle, pushing, shoving, bouncing off dancers twice her size.

Everything inside him pinged, his adrenaline rushing.

Oh, he'd *known,* just known, that his fifteen-year-old sister had no business at a Vonya concert, which was why he'd heard himself volunteering to take her when she appeared in a black-and-purple scoop-neck T-shirt, enough silver costume jewelry to sink a small ship, and skintight animal-print jeans.

And since when had his all-things-Catholic mother decided to say yes to the nose piercing? Clearly, he wasn't the only one who'd lost his mind.

Then again, his mother wouldn't be the first person to let someone talk her into something against her best judgment.

Only, *her* concessions didn't get people killed.

"You don't want to go to a Vonya concert," his sister had whined, shortly after his mother had tossed him the keys to her Subaru, more than a little relief in her eyes.

"I don't care about this Vonya chick—I care about you. Are you sure you don't need a…jacket? Or maybe a paper bag?"

Lucy shot him her best death-ray glare. "I'll just pretend I'm a celebrity. You can be my bodyguard."

"You know, I do sometimes bodyguard people for a living. I might know a few things about staying out of the way."

"Not at a Vonya concert," Lucy said. "I hate to tell you this, dude, but you're in way over your head."

Clearly. He kept his gaze on her as she bounced in the center of the mosh—

She went down.

"Make a hole!" Brody shoved toward her, his blood hot in his veins. By the time he reached her, Lucy had surfaced, her face flushed, holding her nose. Blood dripped out between her fingers.

Okay, that was *it*. He glanced once at Vonya, saw her riding the wave, then wrapped his hand around Lucy's arm. "We're leaving." The so-called music ate his voice.

She yanked her arm away. "I'm fine!" Her painted eyes glittered.

He didn't have time to retort because the punk next to Lucy turned on him. "Leave her alone, dude!" He then threw his body—or perhaps someone threw him—against Brody.

Brody caught him, pushed him away.

Definitely time to egress.

He glanced once more at Vonya, his gut tight, trying to shake off the dread. With a gulp, the pit swallowed her whole.

See? Someone should have stopped the madness long before this.

The crowd swelled around her, people pushing, chaos breaking free, bodies tumbling, screaming ripping through the club.

"Brody!" Fear showed in Lucy's wide eyes.

Brody wrapped his arms around her, pushing them both out of the crowd. "You okay?"

She nodded, still protecting her nose.

Perfect. So much for bringing his sister home in one piece.

"Go to the bathroom and get cleaned up. Stay away from the crowd!" He had to shout inches from her face, but even as Lucy nodded, his attention pulled back to the mob.

No Vonya. But screams and grunts emitted over the microphone, and even the band members had stopped playing.

"Go!" he yelled to Lucy, and plowed back into the violence.

Another elbow to the gut nearly blew out his breath, but he moved with the purpose of a ground assault, shoving bodies aside, protecting his face as he waded through to Vonya's last known position.

Nothing, although he did manage to haul to their feet two women and a very skinny kid.

He made it all the way to the man-size speaker…and spotted a flash of pink huddled behind the equipment.

Vonya crouched, holding her left arm curled tight to herself. Despite the black makeup, the weird peacock mask, the bright pink Marilyn Monroe-style hairdo, and the scaly leather dress, he recognized a woman shaken.

Not that it took a psychologist to figure it out—her mask hung torn from her face and she stared up at him like he might be the boogeyman.

So he didn't stop to focus, analyze or plan. Didn't stop to think through his actions. Just bent down, slipped his arms around her and swooped her up.

"Hey! What are you doing?" She twisted in his arms, eyes wide.

"What does it look like?" he said into her ear, as he pushed through the hysterical crowd toward the back entrance. "Trying to save your pretty little neck."

"Call 911, tell them things are out of control!" she said, twisting in his arms as if wanting to run back into the mess.

"You should have thought of that before you threw yourself into the audience."

She stiffened. "I'm okay. You can put me down."

"Not quite yet, honey."

But he looked at her then. She seemed more petite up close with her crazy pink hair and false eyelashes, and she swallowed back something that looked like shame.

Then he kicked open the back door and freed them to the alley.

"I said, put me down!"

No problem.

Unfortunately, her words came out timed perfectly for the paparazzi, who got a million-dollar shot of him flinching as she landed an openhanded smack across his face.

Of course she'd been summoned by the senator. Ronie finger-combed her sea-sticky hair as she sat in the back-seat of the limousine, her trench coat tucked around her, trying to chase from her bones the last of the chill from the choppy ferry ride to Martha's Vineyard. Her father's voice on her machine rang in her memory…

"Sounds like you made a real spectacle of yourself this time, Vonya. Your mother and I want a word with you. I'll expect you at the beach house this weekend."

Of course he expected her. But at twenty-eight, she thought she might be strong enough to resist his summons.

Well, she might be if she weren't broke and needing the senator's goodwill in the form of financial backing for her upcoming European tour, aka rescue mission.

She'd saved the text message from the Bishop and now ran her thumb over her cell in her pocket.

Found him.

Thank You, God.

Her throat tightened even as she stared out at the ocean, at the frothy waves clawing the shore. *Please let the senator be in a good mood.*

The limo turned into the long drive toward Harthaven, past the weathered split-rail fencing, the green-carpeted pastures. A couple of her mother's thoroughbreds lifted their heads as if in greeting. The tires ground against the gravel until the car pulled up at the front door.

"Nice to see you again, Miss Veronica," the driver said, as he opened her door.

"You, too, Mr. Henley." She lifted her messenger bag from the seat and stood for a moment in front of the ancestral home, two centuries of age in its weathered cedar shakes. Out of habit her eyes went to Savannah's tiny, empty attic window.

"Veronica, you made it!" Her mother's voice emerged first as she exited the house, crossed the porch and descended the front steps. Ellie Wagner looked about twenty-five, with her long brown hair held back in a ponytail, and her brown riding pants and pink blouse. She held her helmet, with a pair of gloves shoved inside, against her hip. "I was just leaving for a quick ride. I'll be back in time for dinner." She pecked her daughter on the check as she breezed by. "Oh, we'll be dressing for dinner tonight, but your father would like to see you for drinks in the study at six o'clock."

"I don't drink." Never had, really. And never mind that

she hadn't called herself Veronica since her sophomore year in college.

But it didn't matter. Her mother waved her gloves and disappeared around the corner to the stable.

"No problem, Mother, I'm down with that," she said to the brisk island air.

She kept a standard little black dress and a strand of pearls in the closet just for Saturday nights at Harthaven. Her fans wouldn't have a prayer of recognizing her.

Sometimes, after a concert, she didn't even recognize herself.

Six p.m. The hour of execution, when she had to discard herself of all things Vonya and climb back into the expectations of her upbringing. But no one could ever accuse her, Veronica Stanton Wagner, of not knowing how to adapt. She'd eaten Zong Zing with the ambassador to China, challenged the sons of the prime minister of Nepal to a game of Bagh Chal, learned to play the *djembe* from a musical troupe from Ghana, and could speak, although poorly, snippets of Portuguese, thanks to the young wife of the United Nations representative from Brazil.

She could probably manage to behave like a proper lady tonight at dinner. Especially if it meant erasing from her father's recent memory the newspaper photo of Vonya laying her palm across a very handsome, yet downright surly, self-appointed bodyguard after last Saturday's debacle.

Yeah, well, she'd been a victim one too many times of a crazy fan. And one very dangerous stalker. How was she to know he actually wanted to help her?

She could still see his shock as he recoiled, then the

growl that flashed into his eyes as he'd gritted his teeth and set her down.

Stabilized her as she rocked on those lethal five-inch heels.

No, not a fan. Thankfully, he hadn't let loose the words behind the disgust that flashed across his face.

But the derision from the stranger hurt, she had to admit it.

Or not a stranger anymore. Brody Wickham. She'd discovered his name after her frantic manager found them returning from the alley. Tommy D had decided to make him a national—or at least music-industry—hero.

She longed to forget him, hating the way he and his condemnation stuck in her brain. In fact, she thought she'd escaped the claw of shame long ago.

Clearly not. And it didn't help that Brody Wickham cast a steely, almost annoyed image across national airwaves and onto prime-time entertainment shows when he announced that he'd simply been trying to keep her from hurting herself.

Nice.

Except maybe he'd been right. She still sported a greenish-black bruise on her arm.

Oh, given the choice, she would rather have holed up in her SoHo loft this weekend with a bowl of popcorn and her keyboard to work on a new song. But she couldn't rightly beg for money over the phone, or even through email. Senator Wagner wouldn't want to miss the pleasure of staring her down and making her feel fifteen and a failure.

Just once, she'd like to be twenty-eight, smart and beautiful.

But this little excursion wasn't for her. Or even for the senator. And life didn't always hand out choices.

An hour later, Ronie gave a last survey in the mirror—short brown hair curled into tiny ringlets around her head, the barest dusting of makeup, a little lip gloss, a touch of lime eye shadow. She appeared, well, wholesome.

She didn't exactly hate the look.

The smells of a pot roast, or maybe lamb with rosemary, tugged her down the stairs. Stopping off in the kitchen, she sneaked a fresh roll from a basket on the counter, earning a growl from Marguerite, their weekend housekeeper, and tore it into tiny pieces as she walked toward her father's study.

The melodies of Tchaikovsky escaped through the cracked open door. She eased it open.

Tripp Wagner stood with his back to her, an outline of power as he stared out the window overlooking the grounds. Twilight had begun to darken the pond and seep across the grass. Only a glimmer of light sprinkled through the pines that ringed their property. Sometimes she wished they had beachfront property, where they could watch the sun sink like a fiery ball behind the sandy dunes.

"Father?"

"Come in, Veronica."

Ronie stepped inside the study. A desk lamp puddled orange over the leather blotter on the mahogany desk. His briefcase lay on the credenza, under a family picture, now nearly fifteen years old. Ronie barely glanced at it, not really recognizing any of the four of them.

"You can help yourself to a drink." He gestured with

a glass of something amber—bourbon, probably—still not turning from the window.

"I still don't drink alcohol, Father," she said, but moved over to the bar and poured herself a glass of cranberry juice. It helped to have something to hold on to when the senator began his orations.

"Not that anyone would ever know."

She braced herself.

"Sometimes, I can't believe that is actually my daughter making a spectacle of— No. I promised your mother." He sighed, turned and, for the first time, let his eyes rest on her. She stifled a tremble, not because he frightened her—well, not much, anymore—but because she saw in his hazel-green eyes such sadness, it filled her throat with something scratchy and hard.

"Sorry," she mumbled. "It's part of the act."

He looked away, rubbing his thumb along the glass. He nodded. "Have a seat."

Not a request—it never was, so she slipped into the Queen Anne chair against the wall. Her father settled one hip against the desk, his pant leg riding up to reveal a dark sock. He probably hadn't had to change for dinner—he had simply gotten up that morning and dressed in a suit and tie. But they'd all been hiding inside their own costumes since Savannah's death, hadn't they?

He took a breath, and in the gap of space, she wondered if maybe she should go first—a burst of *Father, I need your help* might detour the dressing-down.

Or not. Maybe it would only add ammunition. She took a sip of her juice and balanced it on her lap, staring at the blood-red liquid.

"I want you to cancel your European tour."

Her head shot up, but he already had his hand up to stop her words.

"I'm not trying to interfere with your career, Veronica. But the truth is…I've had some disturbing threats lately, and I'm just not sure that you should be parading around in nightclubs across Europe when there are men out there who'd like to see me dead—or worse, at their mercy."

Her father had always been an epic presence in her life. Even now, he seemed invincible, his hair dark as oil, his face unlined, his shoulders broad. The sigh that shuddered through him shook her again.

"What are you talking about?"

He set his drink on the desk. "As the chairman of the Foreign Relations Committee, I am the one who suggested the embargo on Zimbala. General Mubar has decided that I'm an enemy of his people, and that's putting it kindly. He's made a few personal threats lately, the kind that I should take seriously."

"General Mubar wants to hurt you?"

"General Mubar thinks I'm standing in the way of the United States recognizing his illegal government."

She edged forward in her seat. "You know he's starting to recruit child soldiers, right?" She still had the images from her tour imprinted in her head.

"I know, and that's why I recommended that we establish economic sanctions against Zimbala. And why the general's made a very public pledge to hurt me…and I'm worried that will affect you."

"Why me?"

"After your too-publicized visit there three years

ago, he's convinced you had a hand in influencing my decision."

"But I went as Vonya. There was no connection to you."

"Maybe you think this crazy identity as Vonya hides you, but I'm sure Mubar, just like my colleagues in Washington, has figured out who you are. I don't know for sure, but we can't take any chances." He paused, looked at his drink, then back to her.

His gaze seemed to part her chest, burn it. Finally, "Veronica, no matter how hard you try, you won't be able to sever that connection."

Right. Somehow, she found her voice, although when it emerged, it cracked, and sounded nothing like either of the women she worked so hard to be. "I'm not trying to sever that connection—"

A knock at the door cut into her words. "Your guest is here," Marguerite said.

"Give us a moment, then show him in."

Oh, hallelujah, her father had set her up on a date. Now she could spend the entire evening fighting sleep to the tune of some political discussion or a treatise on a new case before the Supreme Court. Didn't he know by now that she'd never fall for a man he'd handpicked? She wanted a poet, or perhaps a musician—someone who embraced life and wasn't made of stone. "Lawyer or politician, Father?"

He frowned at her, as if he had no idea what she might be referring to. "Business, Veronica."

Whatever. She hoped her "date" didn't expect a good-night kiss. "Listen, I understand your warning, but I can't cancel my tour. The record label already took a chance on me, taking me from an indie band to a regular on the pop charts. I need this tour to keep my momentum. Frankly, even if I wanted to cancel, I couldn't. I'd lose all my deposits and end up owing my firstborn child to the record label."

His face twitched. *Oh, great choice of words, Veronica.* She set her drink on the table. Might as well go for broke, since…she was. "The fact is, I need…I need help."

His right eyebrow went up.

"I'm a little in the red right now."

He folded his arms across his chest, and oh, yes, he had her right where he wanted her.

"I lost a lot with the stock market crash, and then, my accountant made some tax mistakes, and I ended up paying back taxes and penalties—"

"Are you still using your Harvard friend for your accounting?"

"—and Tommy D redid the condo for a photo shoot, and it went way over budget—"

"Did I mention I think he has stretched your image a little far? I don't know why you insist on using your college friends to help your…career, or whatever you're calling your flamboyant—"

"Father, please, Tommy D is a great manager, and this is what it takes to stand out."

"Tommy D'Amico recognized 'sucker' written all over you the second he saw you serving at the Harvard Square Homeless Shelter. I think you need to look a little closer at why your money seems to be vanishing."

"I'm not a fool for wanting to help people, Father."

"But you've become a fool doing it."

She stared at her juice, suddenly seeing again her so-called rescuer's disgust.

Her father sighed, turned back toward the window. "So, you need money."

She fought for her voice. "I'm good for it—you know that. I just…well, we put a lot into this tour already and I can't back out. I was hoping…"

She winced. Okay, really, she felt sixteen, and begging for the car keys. How did she ever talk herself into believing this was a good idea?

But to her surprise, he began to nod, a gleam in his eye, something she'd seen too many times when he knew he had her cornered. Oh, no… "I think we can work something out."

"Really?" She hated how she nearly lunged at his words.

He got up from the desk and walked over to the door. "I predicted that you would be averse to my suggestion to cancel, so I was prepared with a counteroffer. Which, I think, might be a win for both of us. Veronica, you can go to Europe on my dime, on one condition."

Her stomach tightened with a sick feeling. "What?"

He opened the door. "Come in, please." Then he backed away, wearing a smile that she'd seen on his campaign posters. "I'd like you to meet your new bodyguard."

Her father's henchman stepped up to the door, six-foot-plus of solid muscle, now dressed in a pedestrian suit, his dark, curly hair combed and tidy, his familiar, unforgiving eyes on her, looking serious, powerful and made of stone.

She let a groan escape. "Oh, no." See? Solid proof that, cosmically, she would never get on God's good side.

"Brody Wickham," he said, holding out his hand. He smiled, looking nothing like the scowler she'd met in the dark alley outside the D.C. club. Then—and frankly, she should have expected his sarcasm—he asked, "Have we met?"

TWO

"Have we met?" Her words, repeated back to him, came out almost like a whisper, her big hazel-green eyes gulping him in as she slipped her hand in his. It took him a second—as her fingers closed around his hand—to realize that she was mocking him. "Very funny," she said without a smile.

He stared at the girl, short brown hair in tight ringlets around her head, a slim black dress, a cultured strand of pearls at her neck, and tried to place her.

"Uh…I'm serious. You father said we'd met, but I don't remember…" He slipped his hand from hers, casting a look at Senator Wagner. "Sir?"

Senator Wagner embodied everything Brody's father had described—serious, a Harvard lawyer, a three-term senator with a hearty knowledge of foreign policy. He exuded the same aura of power that Brody once had while commanding his squad. Only now, a strange expression played on the senator's face.

"You don't recognize the woman you rescued the other night, Mr. Wickham?"

Brody turned back to his newest client, peering at her even as she stepped back from him. And then, he saw it.

The slight hesitation, coupled with the hint of frown not unlike the one the crazy pink-haired rock star displayed right before she'd left her handprint on his cheek.

"Vonya? Seriously?" Oh, no.

"You're kidding me, right?" She looked first at Brody, then her father, and he couldn't figure out whom she might be talking to. "You want *him* to be my bodyguard?"

"That's right. You two already know each other, and I did a background check. Mr. Wickham here works for an international security firm out of Prague. He's a former Green Beret, and he's got the experience I'm looking for—"

"*You're* looking for? What about me? Do I have any say in this?" She stared back at Brody but his instincts told him to just keep his mouth shut. Not that she would let him speak. "Vonya" had begun to materialize via the sarcastic, exasperated tone. "You're holding me hostage. No wait—this is *blackmail*." But as she turned to her father, Vonya morphed back into this strange, almost breakable woman with pleading eyes. "Listen, I *will have* a bodyguard. But I want to pick him—especially if he's going to shadow all my concerts."

"Not just during your concerts, Veronica, but every moment, 24/7. I'm not letting General Mubar—or even last year's crazy stalker, if we really have to go there— find you in the halls of the hostels you and your crew insisted on staying in last time."

"Nonprofit housing, Father, and everything I do to help them goes to help the homeless in Europe. It was part of the tour hype, and where I got my first fans. I can't desert them. I'm just as safe there as I would be in a Hyatt. What is he going to do? Sit outside my door as I sleep?"

"If I have to," Brody said. But to start out, he'd just affix a security system onto her accommodations, and if anyone went in or out, he'd know. A room next door, or across the hall, would be just fine.

And there would be no youth hostels on this pleasure cruise. At least he and the senator agreed on that much.

Even if, right now, everything inside him screamed to turn and run from this room, this mansion, and back to his parents' humble ranch home on the verge of being owned by the bank.

And it happened to be precisely that thought—his parents, homeless, after feeding nine children and working their fingers to the bone—that kept him rooted to the floor.

It was bad enough that Derek planned on joining the military rather than pursuing his basketball scholarship. Who turned down a partial ride to Duke?

Their conversation while they'd been playing a little one-on-one in the driveway—the one that ended with him nearly shouting at his brother—rushed back to him. *"Over my dead body."* He hadn't been sure where his anger came from, but with everything inside him, and more, he knew his brother wasn't giving up Duke to throw his future away in the military.

Derek had stared at him, an openmouthed gape that Brody probably could have predicted. It wasn't like he'd ever dissed the military before.

And, up until a year ago, he wouldn't have stood in his brother's way. But the days of fighting his fellow man had vanished. Now, wars were fought against grade-schoolers with guns and idealistic teenagers with bombs strapped to their bodies. In the villages and homes of innocent women and toddlers. No way would he let his brother be caught in the middle of that.

A guy simply didn't heal from those kinds of wounds. "No way," he'd said.

"You love the military. What's your deal?"

"Join ROTC, become an officer. But no, you're not joining up to be a grunt."

"It's not up to you," Derek said, reaching for the ball.

And the only thing that saved them both had been Senator Wagner on the other end of the cell phone, rescuing Brody from losing it at his brother and saving their financial hide at the same time.

Talk about his instincts misfiring.

"You didn't tell me that your daughter was 'Vonya,' Senator, when you asked me to protect her." Indeed, Brody had imagined some cultural princess who needed her bags carried as she sashayed down the Champs-Élysées. Maybe he'd done the math too quickly—a hundred grand would keep his brother out of the military, at least in the short term, and give him a head start on his future. The kid could change the world, maybe, someday. And paying off his parents' loan could ease Brody's pain at seeing his father struggling to move around the house, trying to recover from his stroke.

"What did you think? I did mention a musical tour."

Violins. Beethoven. A gig with a snooty cellist, perhaps. It was possible—right now, Veronica looked like she could wield a cello while being a spokeswoman for the Daughters of the American Revolution, or perhaps standing next to her father on the campaign trail.

"You didn't mention crazy," Brody said, and enjoyed, probably too much, the gap-mouthed glare from Veron—Von—whoever.

"My security check suggested you could handle this."

Clearly, the good senator had checked into his decorations, his medals, his commendations—but hadn't bothered to talk to Chet. His boss would be over the desk, throttling him if he knew Brody had practically cannonballed back into work. Thankfully, Chet had probably turned off his cell phone when he and Mae had escaped for their honeymoon.

And what Chet didn't know wouldn't hurt him, right? Brody would return to the office in Prague after a month, mandatory R & R accomplished, having outfitted his family with a better future. Seemed like the perfect way to shake free of his demons.

Not if Veronica had her way. "Father, how about a female bodyguard? I mean, after all, I'm going to do some shopping—"

"I'm sure Mr. Wickham can shop."

Um…

"He doesn't even like my music! You should have seen him the other night. He looked like he'd eaten a gourd of *morsick!*"

Nope, he hadn't. African *morsick*—fermented goat's milk in a charcoal-lined gourd—was a lot, or, okay, a little worse than listening to her so-called music.

"He doesn't have to like your music, Veronica. He's getting paid to keep you safe."

Veronica, Vonya, whoever—Brody was searching for any physical resemblance to the flamboyant sci-fi character he'd seen on the stage in this Miss Culture and Pearls—turned and stalked toward the window. She stared out of it, hard jawed. "I don't want him. Pick *anyone else* but him."

For the first time since Brody entered the room, Senator Wagner frowned, pursed his lips, and cast a look at Brody as if considering her request. Like Brody might not be a great fit for his daughter, regardless of her wacky persona.

Her words bothered Brody, too. Why *not?*

Even if he didn't want to babysit Vonya the Superstar, Veronica the Sorority Girl's attitude was starting to get on his nerves. He'd done close protection on more important subjects than the Chameleon over there. "What's the problem?"

She rounded on him, her eyes flashing. "Because, Mr. Wickham, you are a jerk. Without asking, you decided I needed rescuing—"

"You were hiding underneath a speaker!" His gaze flicked to the bruise on her arm, a bloom of pain that probably hurt when she moved it.

"It doesn't matter. I had everything under control, and when I told you to put me down you ignored me."

"Because you were being stupid."

She closed her mouth, opened it, her eyes flashing.

Well, she was. "Sorry, but you were *crawling* across the stage, and then you flung yourself like a Frisbee into the crowd. I had to pluck you out of a *mosh* pit. Of course you were in over your head, and if you don't see that, then we're in worse shape here than I thought." Was he yelling? Not yet, but he wanted to. Now he fully recognized Vonya, if only by the feelings she'd churned up in him.

"Says you."

"Yeah, and about sixteen years of instinct." And at least one act of poor judgment he vowed never to repeat. "Putting you down would have caused a riot. I did what was necessary."

"Without a thought to how *I* might feel."

"So shoot me. I thought you might actually be *grateful* that someone was looking out for you."

He could agree he'd been a jerk, but right now he just wanted to fold his hands around her delicate neck and throttle her. No wonder her father had called him. She reminded Brody too much, suddenly, of Lucy. If she ever acted like this, he'd throw her in a barrel and nail it shut.

Maybe feed her through the hole. Or not.

Okay, that was a little extreme, but the thought of spending one hour, let alone one month, with this woman had him breaking out in hives.

Her eyes narrowed, just for a second. Then, "I don't need anyone to look out for me."

"Your father thinks you do."

She flinched, then looked away, her voice tumbling low. "You don't even like me."

"I don't have to like you to do my job."

Her chin quivered, just slightly, before she turned her back to him.

His chest burned, right in the center. What did it

matter if he liked her? He shook his head, shot a glance at the senator, his voice tight. "Maybe she's right, sir. Maybe you should find someone else."

Maybe he could take out a loan for the house, the tuition…

The senator picked up his drink, considering it for a moment, swishing the liquid in his glass tumbler.

Brody opened his mouth to recant when Senator Wagner cut him off.

"Nope. It's Mr. Wickham or the tour is off." He directed his words to Veronica, who whirled around, her mouth open just long enough to give her away. Then her eyes went to Brody and he saw something flicker in them. Something that looked dangerously like determination.

Was she hiding something? But in a flash, up went a new mask—not quite cultured Veronica, but too serious to be Vonya. A new, probably more charming, personality. Nice.

"Fine. That's just fine. Mr. Wickham will do. As long as he listens to me and stays out of my way." She took a breath and moved toward him. Brody held out his hand again, as if to seal the deal, but she brushed past him.

"Staying out of your way might be a little difficult. And, by the way, just for the record, I do like you," he said, hoping to throw some cool on her steam.

"Save it," she snapped, and shut the door behind her with a click.

Brody blew out a long breath.

The senator clamped him on the shoulder. "Keep her out of the tabloids, keep her out of trouble, and bring her home in one piece. I'm afraid this time you're going to have to earn your pay, Wickham."

Her "bodyguard" pre-cut his roast pork into geometric cubes the size of dice. He speared one piece of meat, pushed it through his applesauce, and delivered it to his mouth. He laid down his fork and wiped his mouth between bites, following each one with a sip of water.

Like a robot.

Ronie tried not to stare, but the more he did it, the more she longed to launch across the beautifully attired table and pour something, maybe gravy—which he'd poured into the center of a perfectly indented mound of potatoes—over his entire plate.

Heaven forbid the gravy touch his asparagus. Or the applesauce.

Or one of Marguerite's rolls, buttered nicely on the bread plate.

Her father had sold her out to a cyborg. The Terminator.

A terminator that just might destroy everything if she wasn't careful. She had better figure out a way to ditch him if she hoped to help Kafara.

Found him. She would reread the text until it gave her the courage she needed.

Brody took another sip and politely answered the senator's questions, in a voice low and rumbly, like an earthquake. "I'm the oldest of nine, sir, and yes, my father worked at the Capitol as a security guard until his stroke three months ago. Nearly did thirty years."

"I know him—gives away your mother's homemade caramel corn to all the offices every year."

Another cube of meat, another trek through the applesauce. Chew. Wipe. Drink. Yes, sitting across from him for the next month just might drive her insane.

Except, well, what about that idea? She couldn't exactly fire him, right? But what if he quit? What if she simply played on his disgust and drove him insane?

Sorry, but she just didn't buy the whole "you're in danger" spiel. Did her father think she had lost her brains along with her pride? He just didn't want another go-round with the international tabloids during an election year. And as for her so-called stalker, well, just because a few unauthorized photos showed up on the internet didn't mean the man would harm her.

Everyone just calm down. She knew what she was doing.

Although she could admit to being just a little terrified when she found herself on the floor of the club. Being stomped on.

Not that Brody would ever know that.

But she would have survived. It was the one thing she knew how to do.

"And what do you do when you're not standing guard outside someone's hotel room?" Ronie tried to smile, aiming for too sweet when she said it.

He met her eyes. "I work out. And listen to classical music." No return smile.

Ellie passed him the rolls. "Isn't that lovely. Our family has season tickets to the New York Philharmonic. We just heard them play Brahms, the Second Symphony."

Ronie wanted to nod off into her potatoes. Maybe a date, forced or otherwise, would have been better—at least said suitor might be trying to impress her father, and her, in hopes of winning round two.

Brody Wickham didn't seem at all interested in her opinion of him.

Well, except for the moment she'd caught him staring, his gaze lingering on her as he'd pulled out her chair to the table.

As if trying to recognize in her the woman who'd belted him.

Yeah, well, there was more where that came from if he got too close. But, see, that could work, too—more craziness, and perhaps she *would* throw in shopping and nightclubs, drive him insane by making him fetch her coffee and donuts, anything she could do to remind him that, yes, she might just be the high-maintenance diva he'd scooped off the floor.

He'd rue the day he ever agreed to her father's terms. If he thought she was hard to control onstage…

"How long have you been in the military, Mr. Wickham?" her mother asked.

Ah, the woman had caught him midbite. Ronie raised an eyebrow, enjoying the debate in his eyes. Finally, he replaced his fork, fully loaded, onto the plate. "I'm not in the military anymore, ma'am. But I was in for sixteen years."

"Only four years shy of retirement? That seems a strange time to leave."

Of course, the senator had to press. Why not? It seemed his specialty had become evaluating people's lives, making them rethink their decisions, embarrassing them…

Brody's gaze went to his plate. Finally, he picked up his fork. "Yes, sir."

Hmm. The silence after his words had even Ronie clinking her plate with her fork, dividing her asparagus into chunks.

Outside, twilight had descended, shaggy fir trees shifting shadows into the yard, and the cicadas had come out, buzzing in the night. Ronie longed to push away from the table and escape outside into the sultry, thick air, slip off her shoes, feel her toes in the cool grass. If she listened hard, perhaps she'd hear laughter from the playhouse on the far edge of the yard, maybe even see Savannah beckoning to her from the swing set.

Not the Savannah that peered down upon them from the oil on the wall behind her in the dining room, but the one with long brown hair, so soft for braiding, the one who knew all the voices to *Little Women*.

"So, I suppose you visited a lot of interesting places in the military?" Ellie to the rescue, still trying to pawn off the rolls.

"Yes, ma'am." Brody accepted another roll, set it next to his already cut and buttered one. What, was he going to slip it into his pocket for later?

"Have you seen action?"

"Oh, Ellie, don't ask him that."

"Yes, ma'am," Brody said, again that strange glance down at his dinner. The entire affair felt not unlike a KGB interrogation. They just needed the bright lights and the toothpicks. For a second, Ronie had the urge to rescue him.

Thankfully, it passed.

"Mr. Wickham's offices are in downtown Prague,

Ellie." The senator turned to Brody. "Beautiful city, Prague. Went there on my twenty-fifth anniversary, with my wife."

Ellie looked over at him with a smile, not a hint of warmth in her eyes. "Yes. Very beautiful."

Her father had finished off his bourbon and switched to merlot. He swished his wine by the stem of the glass. "I saw that you worked for Hans Brumegaarden. Something about a birthday party, and Snow White?"

Was that a blush on Wickham's face? Maybe, but then it vanished and he caught Ronie's eye, straight on. "Yes. Our security firm was asked to dress the part while protecting Gretchen Brumegaarden during her Disney-themed birthday party. I was a dwarf. I'll do anything to keep a client safe. Even if she is five years old and dressed up in some crazy costume."

What? No, he didn't just call her a five-year-old, did he? Her mouth opened. Oh, she so had words for him. But no, she was a Wagner. She'd keep it to herself.

At least tonight.

"I need some air." She pushed away from the table. "Thank you for dinner. I'll see you all in the morning."

Brody rose from the table. The senator stayed seated. Ellie put out her hand, catching her arm. "Veronica—"

"It's Ronie, Mom. My friends call me Ronie. Or, if you want, Vonya would work, too." She pulled away and glanced at the Boy Scout. "The tour starts in a week. Try to stay out of my hair until then."

She was turning away when she heard him mutter, "Which hair?"

And oh, she shouldn't have, but she couldn't stop

herself. In fact, yes, she turned right about five years old as she picked up one of the rolls and hurled it across the table, right at his smug little kisser.

"Veronica!"

He caught it with one hand.

Smiled.

Nodded.

Game on.

Fine. If that was how he wanted it. She turned, ignoring her mother's hand as it tried to catch her.

The moon had lifted above the trees, a spotlight in the sky, skimming over the cool grass. She toed off her sandals, sifting the grass through her feet as she treaded over to the swing set.

She sat on it. Heard the voices of the past.

"When I grow up, I'm going to be a famous actress." Savannah's voice filtered from the yellow playhouse, its windows like eyes, dark and empty. *"I'll sing, too—we'll sing together."*

"Trouble, trouble, I've had it all my days; it seems like trouble going to follow me to my grave."

Ronie pulled her cell phone from her pocket and opened her picture file. She scrolled through the thumbnails, intending to stop on Savannah.

Instead, she clicked open Kafara's picture. Chubby, dark cheeks, a white smile, holding out a pineapple for her right before he cut it in half with his machete. How he loved to bring her treats from his village. She ran her thumb over the photo. *Don't give up on me, Kafara. Because I'm not giving up on you.*

She pocketed the phone, found a tune, something from the past. Let the wind take her song.

"Which hair?" Brody's smug expression, especially after he'd caught the roll, made her push off, start to swing.

Game on, indeed. Yes, he would rue the day he'd agreed to stand in her way.

THREE

Brody Wickham didn't run from crazy. He didn't care what costume Vonya appeared in, what outrageous request she made of him. Didn't care how many times she asked him for a macchiato coffee or food from the craft table. He'd keep on informing her he wasn't a butler—he hadn't been hired to carry her shoes or protect her delicate skin from the harsh sunlight.

And to think the gig hadn't even officially started, although the week spent in New York City watching her rehearse had him second-guessing this gig every day. He couldn't wait for the weekend leave when he'd return to D.C. and check in on his family before leaving for Europe.

Brody Wickham fully planned to outlast her. Figure her out. Win at whatever game they happened to be playing in her head. After all, how was he supposed to protect her if he couldn't predict her moves? She certainly wasn't going to make it easy by, say, cooperating.

She made him want to bang his own head against something hard and cold. Whose brain-dead idea had it been to earn a quick 100K anyway?

"Thank you, Brody." His mother's face when he

handed her a portion of the prepayment of services after returning from the meeting with Senator Wagner. He hadn't expected it to feel so good to help his parents.

Or to know that they wouldn't lose the family home.

Or give his brother a shot at a decent education.

And, truthfully, Ronyika—as he'd taken to calling her—did intrigue him.

After all, he'd never seen anyone wearing giant wings during a pop song before, even if watching her dangle fifteen feet on a trapeze swing off the ground as if she might be flying nearly gave him chest pains. Today her hair was baby-boy blue, an almost clownish mop of curls atop her head. And she wore a black Batman mask, perhaps just in case anyone mistook her for the sugarplum fairy.

In truth, she scared him a little with how quickly she morphed from high-society Veronica to Vampy Vonya.

"Is she schizophrenic? Maybe suffering from multiple personality disorder?" He hadn't exactly meant to say that aloud, but perhaps his disbelief at watching her suspend herself from the ceiling as the fog machine filled up the stage simply overtook his brain and he accidentally went audible with his opinion.

Her manager looked up at him and shook his head. "No, she's brilliant."

"Tommy D" D'Amico reminded him of a man who might greet him at a frat party. Or a used-car sales lot. A full head of blond curly hair, eyes that didn't retain his quick smile, the fast handshake. Shiny alligator shoes that probably cost half Brody's yearly income. What had Senator Wagner said about someone skimming her profits?

Brody had done a background check on Tommy first, followed by Leah, her pretty assistant. If the black-haired whirlwind gained about sixty pounds of muscle and grew a foot, she just might give Brody a run for his money with all the hovering she did.

Although Miss Ronyika hadn't seen anything yet.

But why was a girl who'd been stalked—in and out of the tabloids—uninterested in having a bodyguard?

More intrigue.

He'd kept his distance this week as he conducted his background checks, went over the accommodations— he'd changed them to decent hotels, thank you very much—and scoured the itinerary. If she wanted to be treated like the pop sensation she was becoming, she needed to start thinking about more upscale lodging, venues…perhaps even attire. But he wasn't touching that.

He'd conceded, also, to the fact he'd have to involve the rest of the Stryker International crew—Artyom and Luke—if he wanted to prepare for contingencies at the concert venues. Thankfully, the Stryker staff jumped at the work, also bored with their mandatory R & R.

Now if he could just figure out Vonya's mind. It was not unlike trying to get a firm grip on Jell-O.

"You know she did two years in Harvard's MBA program for international business, right? And can speak four languages? She's a genius with this stuff."

Really? Because how much genius did it take to sing "Your love gives me wings, makes me sing, on a swing"?

Still, four languages? Could one of those possibly be Klingon?

"I have to admit, she looks like she could just about fly if she wanted to." He winced, however, at how high she swung. Hopefully the grips would make sure the trapeze was secure, or he would. She might be hard to catch.

"The wings are her design, as is the swing act. It'll be a hit." Tommy patted him on the arm as the director stopped the scene. The recorded music died in the speakers.

An air-conditioned chill collected in the warehouse, despite the tepid June air outside. Vonya must be freezing in her light blue leotard and tights. However, she seemed the consummate professional, hitting every cue. And, if someone put him under the bright lights, he might even admit that she exuded a sort of Marilyn Monroe beauty that wasn't completely unlikable.

Tommy clapped as she finished her song, the stage crew lowering the swing so she could hop off. "But you're right, no one can pull off the wings like Vonya. We'll add in the special effects for the video and sweep at this year's MTV Awards." He turned to Brody, white teeth showing. "You're the lucky one—you get to watch her premiere the live act as part of the tour."

Oh, yes, lucky him.

"She won two awards last year, you know. One for a music video, and she was up for best album, too. A real coup for an indie band. But she's headed toward the big-time—even international stardom with this tour." Tommy D shook his wrist, checking his diamond-encrusted watch, shiny under the spotlights. "I just hope you're up to this."

Brody raised an eyebrow.

"I mean, the last bodyguard her father hired ended up in the hospital. Heart attack."

Really? Brody nearly put his own hand to his chest watching her swing in the air.

"Heart attack, huh?"

"The first time we were in Zimbala. She had just walked into a refugee camp. Of course, the man spent more time at the craft table than in her shadow, but yes. Heart attack. Could have been much worse." Tommy patted him again, a habit that just might cause him to lose a hand. "But she's not on any goodwill trips this tour, so probably you're okay."

"Goodwill trip?"

"Oh, it's Ronie's weakness—she's got the heart of Mother Theresa. Can't pass up a child in need. We have to visit every refugee camp, every orphanage. But I told her, no bleeding-heart stunts this time."

Yes, he'd read that, but honestly, he thought it more publicity than fact. She intrigued him, this woman of numerous personalities—and, apparently, layers.

After she had left the dinner table the other night, he'd spied her in the yard nearly an hour later, swinging on an old swing set, humming.

She'd seemed so forlorn, for a crazy second he'd almost pitied her. After all, even he had felt the chill at the dinner table between Mrs. and Senator Stuffy. It didn't take a psychologist to see open wounds.

Not that he could hide his so much. He remembered

more staring at his cold pork roast than was good for him.

Maybe, suddenly, he understood the Vonya act, just a little.

He took another sip of his black, industrial-strength coffee. "Listen, Tommy, I need to know if she's going to do any more crazy stunts like she did at the D.C. club."

"Like?" Tommy D raised an eyebrow.

"Like throw herself into the audience? Maybe climb on top of a speaker and dive? I mean, look at her—she's flying. I think she's got a Superman complex."

Indeed, now that the stage crew had finished lowering her to the stage, she balanced atop a baby grand.

"She's a bird—you know, flying?" Tommy shook his head. "You bodyguard types haven't a creative bone in your body."

Hello, but yes, he did. Just…okay, he liked his creativity confined to Sunday morning omelets.

"Just how creative is she? I mean, do I have to watch out for her turning into a clubbing diva and sneaking out to paint the city?"

Tommy's mouth quirked. "I don't think you have anything to worry about. She'd rather stay in her hotel room and hang out with Lyle."

Lyle?

But Tommy moved away, shouting directions at the director.

Lyle. Brody tried to ignore the *Idiot!* ringing in his head for not knowing about her boyfriend. He took another sip of coffee, already mentally texting Artyom for a background check. Just when he thought he'd crossed all his *t*'s.

It was this kind of oversight that got people killed.

He watched as she crossed her blue legs and leaned forward, puckering her lips. A photographer grabbed the shot.

Anyone who could keep up with Vonya's attention span must be an interesting guy. Brody took another sip of coffee, then threw it in the trash, reaching for his phone.

Artyom texted him back almost immediately, apparently holed up in a hotel in Berlin while Luke met with the security team at the Klub, Vonya's Berlin venue.

How are the Prague and Amsterdam venues?

All set in Prague. Heading to Amstdm next.

Brody closed his phone. Vonya had hopped off the piano, helped herself to juice and was leaning against the wall, possibly reading her mail on her iPhone.

Like a normal person. She just might be the most gifted master of disguise he'd ever met, because she appeared comfortable in every persona she donned.

But she hadn't trusted him enough to tell him about Lyle, had she? Clearly, if he hoped to get her to open up, to let him truly protect her, he'd have to play her game.

"You don't even like me."

The words pinged inside him for some reason.

He wasn't paid to like her. But if he had to pretend to get her to cooperate, well, no one ever accused him of not being willing to sacrifice for his job.

And he wasn't exactly lacking in the charm department. He'd had his share of women on his arm.

He pocketed his phone, swung by the table, filled a plate with grapes and cheese, and brought it over to her.

She looked up at him, and for a moment, the sadness in her blue-painted eyes stopped him cold. Were those—

Yes. She lifted her hand to swipe it across her cheek, then stopped herself and blinked the tears away. He could recognize a forced smile when he saw it. "Can I help you?"

Wow, he wanted a glimpse of what might be on her screen that would elicit that response. "You need to eat." He handed her the plate and leaned over a bit.

She stared at the food plate as if it might be a bomb. "What's this?"

"Grapes. And I think that's Gouda."

She considered him a moment, then glanced at the phone. "Uh…"

"I can hold that for you."

She moved her thumb over the screen, then handed over the phone and took the plate. "Thank you?"

He nodded, smiled. "You're welcome."

"It doesn't mean we're friends, you know." She picked up a grape, popping it in her mouth.

"Heaven forbid." He glanced at the phone. She'd closed out her screen, of course.

"I wanted to ask you about Lyle."

She raised one eyebrow, popping another grape into her mouth. "Lyle? Why?"

"Apparently he's an important part of your life. I think I need to meet him, especially if he's going to be hanging around during the tour." That was nice and casual, not a hint of annoyance in his voice that she hadn't even once mentioned the man.

"I'm not sure he's going. Leah hasn't decided yet."

What did her assistant have to do with her boyfriend's decision to join her? "Why not?"

"He's got school."

Lawyer? Doctor? He didn't exactly know why this bothered him. "What is he studying?"

A slow smile slid up her face, almost like a shark pulling back its teeth. "Gym and lunch are his favorite subjects, I think." At this, she winked and finished off the last of the grapes. "I'll make sure he stops by later. I do think it's time you met my son." She handed him the plate and took back her phone, leaving him standing there with a big pile of stinky cheese.

Oh, the look on Brody's face had been priceless. So worth accepting his goodwill grapes.

Even if, technically, she'd had to lie. Although she *considered* Lyle her son. He'd been living with her every summer and holiday since she'd found the four-year-old curled up on the park bench her freshman year of college at Columbia University where she did her undergraduate work.

Which, of course, led to her meeting his sister, Leah. And arranging for his schooling with their mother, at least until the day the cops found her dead in Central Park.

Now Leah had official custody.

And Brody had looked like she'd belted him again.

See, no one pulled a fast one on Vonya.

"Ronie, are you okay in there?"

Ronie could picture Leah just outside the door, her kinky black hair wild around her face, dressed in a peasant's shirt, tied at the neck. Leah's appearance, head to toe, matched her personality—friendly, fun, honest. She'd turned into an exceptional assistant, and Ronie couldn't imagine a Sunday morning without pancakes with her and Lyle.

Ronie wiped her face, toweled off her hair. "I'll be out in a minute. How did your interview go with Brody Wickham, aka the Boy Scout?" She wiped the mirror with a washcloth, a swipe as large as her hand that revealed her streaked, formerly made-up face. Rehearsals for her tour seemed even more grueling today, and instead of showering at the studio, she'd raced home to her own digs.

"Wick—that's his nickname. He seems nice. And genuinely concerned for your safety."

"Yeah, too concerned if you ask me." She would need another layer of remover to wipe the last of the indigo blue from around her eyes, but finally, she'd begun to see hints of her real self. Unremarkable hazel-green eyes, brown hair chopped short, the color of prairie mud, now knotted in a mass from a brisk towel-rubbing. A few freckles formerly concealed with powder. And pale yet plump lips that others probably envied, but on her it looked like too much effort for too little result.

"This coming from the woman who still winces when she moves her arm."

Ronie lifted her left arm, letting the mirror reveal the purple-black bruise encircling the top of it. It still hurt to move it; tears still sprang to her eyes when someone bumped it.

"There's no such thing as too concerned. I think Brody Wickham is the real deal. I saw him watching you all day—I'm telling you, if you had slipped from that swing, he has arms that could catch you."

"I think he's just as likely to let me hit the ground."

"He'd take a bullet for you. I can see it in his eyes."

Perfect. Just what she wanted—another person dying because of her.

Okay, yes, maybe she couldn't dislodge him from her brain—especially that smug expression as he tried to catch a glimpse at her phone.

Good thing she'd deleted the text. See, a person shouldn't save text messages on their phones—not in the new age of spy games.

No, she'd just have to keep his attention diverted while she played out her extracurricular activities.

"I thought rehearsals went okay today, didn't you?" She peered in the mirror at her bloodshot eyes, a few gathering wrinkles around her mouth. Okay, she shouldn't be quite so hard on herself. With the right makeup, she could turn the head of a photographer. At least as Vonya.

"I think you're brilliant. I love the swing song."

She thought it was one of her cheesier pieces, but the crowds loved it. And Vonya vamped it up well, although it was one of the few songs that felt most like one Ronie might sing. All the same, it didn't matter what persona she played onstage, as long as it opened doors. As Vonya she'd held a concert for the troops overseas, she'd raised money for UNICEF, she'd visited the refugee camps in Africa…

All, of course, Tommy used for the good of her career. She used it for the good of her heart.

And in Zimbala, she'd met Kafara Nimba, a nine-year-old orphaned boy who had captured her heart.

This trip, she'd bring him home.

"Is it okay if I take off? I left the Thai food on the counter. And Tommy said he'd be by later to check on you and go over the itinerary."

Ronie cinched the towel around her and opened the door. "Are you picking up Lyle or am I?"

"I'll go—we'll meet you at the airport on Saturday morning. Listen, you're all packed, you just need to get yourself there on *time*. No more holding the plane while you run through security."

"They didn't believe I was Vonya—what could I do?"

"That's your fault for traveling as yourself."

Yeah, see, no one recognized her when she simply played…herself. Not even her, anymore.

Leah hadn't moved from the door, and Ronie stilled. She closed her eyes when Leah said softly, "I'll be praying for you. For the record, I think you're doing the right thing."

Her feet clicked on the cork floor down the hallway. Ronie pressed her hand to the foggy mirror and pulled it away, watching her handprint. The right thing.

Yes, eventually it would be.

A half hour later, her face scrubbed clean, wearing her green Hulk pajama pants and an oversize Harvard sweatshirt, she found the Thai food in the kitchen in the middle of an otherwise empty countertop.

The entire apartment on the top floor of her building

in SoHo reflected Vonya's eccentric style, thanks to Tommy D's vision for who she should be—at least for the various magazines that wanted an "insider look" into her life. The past year and a half, she'd risen in popularity so much she barely recognized the woman who just loved to write songs in the quiet of her room. From the S-shaped workspace suspended on cables in the middle of the kitchen, to folding Japanese screens that separated the spaces, to the two-story windows overlooking the skyscape of New York, the place exuded the artistic, eccentric flare of Vonya.

The only room Ronie claimed for herself—and she'd practically had to throw her body over it—was the tiny library with the round window that overlooked the rooftops of her neighbors' buildings. Yes, she could be accused of sitting in the darkness, watching people as they stargazed on their rooftops or sometimes serenaded the city. She often grabbed her guitar and played along.

Her library contained her books, a white shag carpet, a chaise lounge she'd picked up at an estate sale and re-covered in lime-green, her old acoustic guitar, and a pile of lined music sheets and notebooks filled with her handwritten songs.

Not that any of them would be sung by Vonya. Even if Ronie did bring them out into the light, they'd die under the bright glare of Tommy D's criticism.

Aw, she didn't really want to be a blues singer anyway, did she?

She'd definitely picked the wrong song to sing on Talent Night at the Harvard Business School. Wow, talk about getting in over her head.

Ronie brought the Thai food to the white sofa, curled up on it, and flicked on the television. She avoided the entertainment and fashion channels, ignored the soaps, and finally settled on a cooking show. Bizarre foods. Could be fun to eat fried squid on a stick, right?

The phone rang and she gave herself permission to let it go to the machine. Probably just Tommy, letting her know he'd be late.

"Veronica Stanton Wagner, this is your father, and if you're there, I expect you to pick up."

Ronie caught a long noodle with her chopsticks.

"Okay, well, I just wanted to say…" He cleared his throat. She paused, her food halfway to her mouth. "Have a good trip."

Oh, see, now that was nice—

"Please try to stay out of the newspapers. And don't drive your bodyguard mad. We've paid him good money to keep an eye on you."

Ronie sucked in a breath.

"And your reputation."

He hung up.

Ronie caught a piece of baby corn. Perfect. Just once, she'd like to hear his daddy voice instead of the senator voice, but frankly, it had been so long she probably wouldn't recognize it.

She stirred her food, then set it down. If only she could have figured out another way to raise money other than go crawling back to her father.

Maybe she shouldn't have given away quite so much of her money to charity. But she couldn't live with herself if she didn't help—after all, she had so much to make up for.

She clicked off the television and stared at the glittering lights of the city, fatigued to the bone.

From inside her messenger bag next to the door, her cell phone buzzed. She put down her carton of food, got up and retrieved it.

A new text message. From Bishop.

Keep your promise, I'll keep mine. Good luck.

It came with an attachment. She opened it, her heart racing.

Kafara. She knew him like her own handprint, despite the grainy image. He stood with three other boys about his age in a field next to a green truck. They wore dirty green pants and black shirts, their eyes dark and solemn.

Gravel filled her throat.

Each one of them held a black-as-night AK-47 on his hip.

She sank to the floor, ran her finger over Kafara's twelve-year-old face. She knew it, she just knew that when his letters stopped, when she'd heard of the raid in his village, that General Mubar had "recruited" Kafara into his private army of enforcers.

Please, God, don't let him have been used for mine-sweeping, or to murder someone.

Her hand shook as she saved the picture to her files. Yes, she'd most definitely have to shake Brody Wickham off her trail, whatever it took.

FOUR

"Derek, I don't suppose you'd consider just picking up your smelly socks, would ya? You're contaminating all my gear. Help a guy out?"

Derek shot him a chest pass and Brody caught the basketball, dropped it once to the pavement, then went up into a jump shot. The ball caught the rim and shot back out like a boomerang.

Derek snatched it from the air. "You're getting rusty."

Or just old. This entire—now shortened—vacation had turned into one giant reminder of how much Brody had missed over the past twelve years living overseas. He'd cut his family out of his life—not intentionally but just by letting work supersede family events. Graduations, weddings, reunions.

Maybe he shouldn't be taking off so soon.

Which was why he scuttled home after rehearsal last night, just in time to see Derek creep into his bedroom after his shift at the local convenience store. With the dark curly hair, the wide shoulders, the lean build— the kid seemed a rubber stamp of himself at the age of eighteen. Now if he could just keep him from becoming the cynical, angry man Brody had turned into. And no amount of praying, or asking for forgiveness, seemed to heal him. Maybe there was no forgiveness for him, despite what his Bible and his faith told him.

A man with scars so deep they touched his bones. And apparently also knocked him off his game. Like yesterday—Vonya had obviously seen right through his attempts to charm her.

If he didn't figure her out, she would have him wrapping himself up in knots.

He and his boys at Stryker International would have to earn every penny of that hundred-thousand-dollar check.

Now if he could simply figure out how to get past her stubborn pride. Or was it something more?

Maybe her so-called sneaky behavior bothered him more than it should. After all, what had she done, really? She certainly wasn't harboring national secrets.

Still, she'd taken way too much pleasure in mocking him about Lyle. He'd done his homework, and she'd lied. *Not* her son. But someone had plunked down a good chunk of cash to pay for this kid's boarding school in upstate New York. He was beginning to see the footprints of Veronica…

He swiped at the ball, but Derek faked and moved around him, going in for a layup.

The ball swooshed through the net and Brody caught it.

Twilight crept through the neighborhood, stirring to life the cicadas, the fragrance of fresh-cut grass. Ten years ago, it would have been the old station wagon parked at the curb in front of his parents' house. Now, a low-budget hybrid, scaled down to transport the only two siblings still at home, lounged next to the curb. And in front of that, Derek's beater Honda.

In fact, too much had changed for Brody to feel completely at home—like his father shuffling around with a walker, trying to get his feet back under him.

Or his mother, dragging home dead tired from her day in the hospital's food service department.

Brody dribbled the ball out past the designated key— the crack down the center of the driveway—then turned and let fly a beautiful three-pointer, right above Derek's outstretched arms.

Swish.

"Pretty," Derek said, grabbing the ball.

"You can take back that rusty comment any time," Brody said, hating that sweat dribbled down his forehead and into his eyes while his kid brother looked as fresh as if he were out for a Sunday stroll.

"Only if you leave my socks alone." Derek brought the ball out past the line and did some fancy dribbling. No wonder the kid was a varsity all-star. "So, what's she like?"

Brody whacked at the ball and missed. "Who?"

"Vonya. I mean, you totally rock, bro. I can't believe you not only met her but actually picked her up and carried her out of that mosh pit. Like, you *touched* her, dude."

Brody knocked the ball from Derek's grip. It shot out into the grass and he chased after it. "Yeah, well, it was no big deal."

Derek didn't move. "Are you kidding me? Every guy

at school has been bugging me for a week, wanting the 411. Did you get her digits?"

Brody scooped up the ball, breathing hard, then finally sat in the grass he'd mowed that morning. "I got hired to protect her during her tour. I've spent the week watching her rehearse. And we leave tomorrow."

Derek flopped down next to him. "Wow. Is she as hot in person?"

In person? Not exactly, but at the senator's house, she did have a sort of class that had stunned him.

In fact, he felt like he chewed on his tongue all the way through dinner at the Wagners'. Until, of course, she pitched the roll in his face. Now, that was a little hot.

No. Not hot—good grief, he sounded like a teenager.

"I don't know. I'm just protecting her."

"Oh, come on, dude."

He still couldn't merge the split screen between Vonya and Veronica. But he didn't especially like either version, thanks. "Naw, she's not my type."

Derek grabbed the ball, spinning it on his finger. "What's not your type? Have you looked at her?"

Brody pushed him over. "Please tell me that you're really not a moron, and I don't have to hurt you. There's more to a woman than how she looks."

"Yeah, sure there is." Derek grinned at him, setting the ball between his knees. "Okay. I'm just kidding. So what's she like?"

"You don't even like me." Again Brody heard pain in her voice. What did she care if her bodyguard *liked* her?

Brody combed through the grass, picking up the

remnant cuttings. "From what I can see, she's totally out of control, flamboyant, stubborn, ungrateful, selfish and a waste of exceptional talent."

Derek smiled at him. "Uh-huh. Wow. Yeah, it's a good thing you're working for her because, you know, you're definitely *not interested*."

Brody glared at him.

"Then again, maybe you don't know how to get a girl's number. It's not like you've been around any women for the past ten years. Last time I checked, they don't let women into Special Forces."

No, not the Special Forces, but he'd been around women.

Or rather, *a* woman.

Brody looked away and, just like that, Shelby was there in his thoughts, her hand over her eyes to keep out the dirt churned up by the chopper, the wind whipping her brown shirt, waving to Brody as he touched down on the dusty pad.

Brody reached for the ball. "I think it's time for a game of Horse."

But Derek was looking at him strangely, as if he'd seen right into his brain. "There was a woman, wasn't there?"

"Seriously, you might have me in one-on-one but I can still outshoot you."

"Who was she?" Derek moved the ball away, out of reach.

Brody pursed his lips. Well, it wasn't like Derek was the CIA, or even a psychologist. "A doctor I met at a refugee camp in Africa. We were evacuating patients and helping with food distribution."

"What was her name?"

"Dr. Shelby Marks." He'd so rarely spoken her name over the past year, just letting it form on his lips elicited ache. And it also had the power to conjure. She lingered in his mind, long blond hair held up in a ponytail, wisps around her face, big green eyes filled with compassion, hands that could heal.

And way too much determination in her expression for her own good. *His* own good.

Especially when that determination had turned into desperation.

"What happened? Did you two break up?"

Brody looked away, toward the bruised sky. "No. We were really never together. I met her, she had something about her—probably I had more feelings for her than she did for me. But we never really found out."

Derek stayed silent beside him.

Brody shook his head, almost willing the words back, but his chest flooded with an urge to tell someone. To breathe it out, with the hopes that in the telling the pain would loosen its hold, even fly into the atmosphere.

"She was killed while trying to rescue one of her patients."

Derek frowned. "I'm sorry." He squinted, as if trying to read Brody, and then—probably because the kid was his spittin' image on the inside as well as the outside— said, "You were there."

Brody sucked in a breath. Nope, it hadn't worked. The pain had returned, filling every pore, burning, shaking through him. "Yeah. She died in my arms."

Derek looked away, following his glance to the darkening horizon.

They sat in silence, listening to the cicadas, the cars motoring home into suburbia. Any moment now, Mom would have a roast on the table. Dinner would be loud and noisy, the perfect escape from this moment. From *every* moment over the past year when the image of Shelby, looking up at him with fading eyes, paralyzed him.

"How'd she die?" Derek asked softly. Brody recognized the compassionate tones of their mother in his kid brother.

Brody's own voice turned hard. "She trusted the wrong people. She heard a woman and her son had left the camp, and she went after them. Such a stubborn woman. I told her not to, but she wouldn't listen to reason. Just had to do it her way."

Brody, for once, will you just follow your heart instead of your head? Emotions did that—put his brain, his common sense, on the fritz. Which was exactly why he'd never let them out of their box again.

"It was a trick. She was ambushed. Shot by a bunch of rebels."

Derek didn't move. "But you took them out."

"Yeah." Brody nodded, his body steeling against his words. "I took them out."

Derek said nothing as he stretched his fingers out over the ball, then held it up in his grip. "Is that why you quit? Why you're doing this mall-cop stuff?"

Although it tore through him and turned him inside out if he let it, Shelby's death wasn't what drove him from his life in the military, just short of his retirement.

It wasn't *her* screams that woke him in a cold sweat in the middle of the night, gasping.

It wasn't *her* blood spilled that made him long for the mindless, easy job as a security specialist for Chet Stryker's international security firm.

She'd known the cost and was ready for it.

But there could never be a healing, a catharsis, a forgiveness for killing ten-year-olds. Even if one of them did have an AK-47 aimed at Brody's head. No wonder God seemed so quiet, although it had been Brody's hope that He would forgive him that kept driving him to his knees, reading the Bible. Hope, however, had started to wane.

So, Brody took a breath, dug deep into his training, and found his decoy voice. "I'm a little more than a mall cop but yeah. I needed something a little less life-and-death."

"I get that." Derek spun the ball. "You ever going to go back, into the military?"

No, he just wanted to lie low, put the pieces together, try to live with himself. He didn't really mind babysitting five-year-old princesses or running security checks on international bankers' vacation homes. Anything to keep his mind off the past, to make him feel like he wasn't a complete failure. "That life's over."

"So is that why you're watching over Vonya?"

Was that why? To keep him from looking over his shoulder, or salvaging his future?

Maybe.

But somehow, over the past week, it had become more. Little Miss Pop Star had all his instincts firing— she had something to hide, and he wanted to know what it was.

Last time he'd ignored his instincts, people died.

Never again. He simply couldn't live with himself if it happened again. Even if she did drive him a little crazy along the way.

"I just hope she's not as much trouble as she seems."

Derek passed him the ball. "I have no doubt that you know what you're doing, bro."

Until recently, he thought he did.

He probably stayed up too late going over the different venues, the staff at the events. Threat assessment with a short deadline seemed sketchy at best, and he hated it.

Someone should have been watching Vonya's back long before this. He'd found no less than three websites dedicated to "Vonwatch," and some of the threads on her fan forums felt downright creepy. Still, even he had to admit that her so-called stalker from last year seemed more of a starstruck fan than a guy out to hurt her. And as for General Mubar's threats…well, he'd threatened half the congress, not to mention the U.S. media and the United Nations.

A small part of Brody might agree he had defaulted to overachiever mode. Still, he was paid to stay on her like glue, whether she needed it or not.

The D.C. sky bled gray as he drove to Reagan National Airport. He dropped his rental car off, then found his flight. Thankfully, he'd booked a window seat. He popped in his earbuds, letting the cool electric blues find him. Stevie Ray Vaughan, God rest his soul, knew how to calm his nerves.

Classical. He smiled at the answer he'd given Veronica at the table. She wasn't the only one with secrets. Only difference—he had every intention of unearthing every last one of hers.

* * *

Brody's plane touched down at LaGuardia and he grabbed a coffee, then headed toward the VIP lounge of their KLM carrier. He'd wanted a charter flight, but Vonya had nixed that. At least he'd managed to secure for them first-class seats.

Okay, he'd secured first class for him and Vonya and Tommy D. The road manager, the band and Leah would fly in business class.

He entered the lounge and spotted a few familiar faces among the travelers. Tommy D raised a Bloody Mary to him, nodding.

Leah sat in a corner, earbuds in, eyes closed.

Where was Ronyika? A businessman tapped out something on his computer. Another was concentrating on his iPhone. A third stood at the bar, ordering up something bracing for the flight.

A woman with a plaid brimmed hat and overlong brown hair tied back in a messy ponytail, wearing yoga pants and pink Uggs, read a Jane Austen book, a pair of black glasses low on her nose.

Ah, there she was. Staring at the tarmac, with blond hair piled up like a long-ago starlet, a red leather jacket over her shoulders, wearing go-go boots and a leather skirt. He dropped his bag into a chair and slid up to her.

"Nice disguise. But you can't fool me."

"Oh, honey, this is the real thing."

The gravelly voice of a lifelong smoker grumbled out the words as the woman grinned at him. Definitely too old for that short skirt. He didn't want to guess further.

She looked past him, turning as the man from the bar offered her something orange and frothy.

Okay, his instincts simply weren't firing anymore. He skulked back to his bag, scanning the room.

An adolescent boy with mocha skin, wearing a pair of skater shoes, jeans and a orange T-shirt, fought with his Nintendo. Another woman, her long legs crossed, flipped a newspaper.

"Where is she?" He looked at Leah, raising an eyebrow. She popped out her earbuds.

"What?"

"Where's—?" This was why he needed his backup. It wasn't like he could announce her name here in the middle of the airport, right?

"Ronie?" Leah said.

"I'm right here."

He turned. The brunette put down her book and grinned up at him. "Gotcha."

Oh, weren't they going to have fun?

She was so going to win their security war. She waited until Brody buckled in next to her, then slipped out past him to the bathroom. They were closing the doors but she had time for a quick text.

I'll be there.

At this rate, Kafara was halfway home.

She deleted her sent message, then adjusted the wig— something Savannah had worn near the end—and smiled into the mirror. *Thanks, sis.*

The flight attendant had begun to read off the passenger instructions as she slipped back into her aisle, climbing over Brody to get to her window seat.

"Listen," he whispered, "we need to come to some agreement here."

She buckled her seat belt, cinching it down, and grabbed *Pride and Prejudice*. "I don't know what you're talking about."

He made a face and shook his head. Ha. She could recognize frustrated when she saw it. Another week, tops, and he'd go packin'.

"Ronie, you win. I quit."

Huh? Already? She turned to him, hating suddenly the feeling of loss. Okay, this had been way too easy. "I win?"

"I can't keep up with your disguises. And you clearly don't want to let me in on your life. I mean, it would have been nice to know that Lyle was going on this trip with us."

She'd seen him back in business class, with Leah, still head-down in his game. "I'm sorry. He was a last-minute addition."

"But one I should have known about. I'm not a bad guy—I get that you want to take him with you. We just need to work on our communication. I'm not the guy who's going to stand in your way. I'm just going to make sure you're alive when you get there."

Brody had pretty eyes. She hadn't really noticed them before—a dark green, almost, with flecks of hazel inside. And he smelled good, too. Like Old Spice cologne. She'd actually noticed the flight attendant's gaze rest on him as he'd lifted her bag into the overhead.

He filled out that black T-shirt pretty well, too.

Not that she was looking. Because, contrary to his

belief, he *would* stand in her way. At least once he found out what this trip was really about.

Still, maybe she could appease him a bit. Get him to lower his guard, offer an olive branch. "Maybe you're right. I have been giving you the dodge, haven't I?"

"A little. And really, you should be a spy or something with the way you can slip into a room unnoticed."

A spy. She tried to stay calm, not let herself give anything away. If he only knew… Still, she let a little smile escape. "Thanks. I spent years perfecting that move at my father's dinner parties. Savannah and I—" She sucked in a breath. "I was always trying to get my hands on a glass of champagne. Until, of course, I succeeded, and managed to throw up all over my Christmas dress. Hate the stuff. I don't drink."

But his smile had dimmed on her Savannah slip. She swallowed past a boulder in her throat. No, please. "What are you listening to?" She reached out for his iPhone and she could have hugged him—okay, not really, but he did win points when he released it to her. She scrolled through his playlist. "Stevie Ray Vaughan, BB King, Otis Rush, Eric Clapton…and Big Joe Turner? You got a great mix of blues here."

He seemed to consider her for a moment. "I was listening to *Texas Flood* on the flight from D.C."

"I'm more of a BB King fan, although I love the cover song for *Texas Flood*. I have the live version on my phone. But I'm more into the original blues. In my other life, I'm Bessie Smith. Or Billie Holiday." She handed him the phone. "I have to admit, I'd never peg you for a jump blues fan."

"That's more for fun." He turned the phone off. "Bessie Smith?"

"My mother had an album. We listened to it all the time when we rummaged through her closet. Savannah…" What was her problem? Why couldn't she seem to get her sister out of her brain? Or her vocabulary? She sighed, letting the sentence play out. "She had a great blues voice. I can still hear her—'Trouble, trouble, I've had it all my days; it seems like trouble going to follow me to my grave.'"

Oh, see, when she let it, the past just took over, and she began to babble. She rolled her eyes, fighting the burn in them. "Sorry."

But his eyes had gone strangely gentle. "She was the fifth person in the room the other night. Can I ask what happened?"

She wouldn't have answered, couldn't have answered, but his voice, low and soft, seemed so…genuine. So willing to listen…to her.

Not Vonya.

Not Veronica.

Shoot, even if it was an act, she couldn't help herself. "Savannah was my older sister, by two years. She died when I was fifteen, from leukemia. Actually, she died because her body rejected my kidney, but probably it had more to do with the lethal combination of antirejection drugs in her body. And the last-ditch efforts…" She lifted a shoulder, turned to look out the window. The plane backed away from the gate.

"I'm sorry."

"It was a long time ago. But sometimes I still miss her."

Oh, why had she said that? Now he'd pat her arm or something, or maybe even start acting—how? It wasn't like she even knew him well enough to guess.

Although suddenly, a part of her wanted to. Especially when he said, "She used to like to swing, huh?"

She turned to him. "How did you know that?"

"You were singing on the swing at Harthaven. It drifted in my window."

He'd been watching her? She let that soak in for a moment before nodding. "She loved to swing. And dress up in our mother's old clothes. And sing the blues." And now she felt as if she'd just opened up her chest for him to take a good peek.

He gave her a long look, finally nodding. "She sounds like someone I would have enjoyed knowing."

The plane engines revved and they taxied down the runway. She had the strange urge to reach over and take his hand.

Like *that* made sense.

The plane leveled off, reached cruising altitude. Ronie turned on her iPod, about to slip in her earbuds, when he leaned over to her. "So, if you love the blues so much, why the pop stuff? How did you get into the Vonya act?"

"Talent Night, my second year at grad school. Tommy D, who was my best friend even then, wanted me to sing. It was for charity—we were raising money for the Harvard Square Homeless Shelter, and since I was involved, I thought, sure, I could sing something. But I just couldn't…"

"You couldn't bring yourself to sing the blues."

She met his eyes, caught inside their compassion too

long. "I came up with a funny song, something Tommy and I put together, then created a costume. It felt easier, you know, to be someone else. I probably overplayed it, and, well, Vonya was a hit. The songs were simpler back then—pop love songs, just for fun. But pretty soon Tommy had me booked in other venues. It sort of took on a life of its own, and in the beginning it was all fun. I gave everything I earned to the shelter, and it gave me a chance to sing. But then Tommy got me a gig on a late-night show, and it was all over from there. I could either finish my master's degree or become Vonya. I thought it would be nice to take a break from school, so I dropped out. I didn't mean for it to go this far, but...I have my reasons."

He seemed to be mulling over her last words. Whoops, maybe she shouldn't have suggested ulterior motives. "Do you write your own music?"

She couldn't stop the smile that quirked the side of her mouth. If he only knew. "I used to. Now Tommy chooses them—we have a stable of songwriters. Only recently, the songs have become a bit..."

"More seductive?"

She bit her lip. "I don't necessarily like my new stuff. But it's Vonya, you know, and..." She lifted a shoulder. "She opens doors."

"You sound like you're playing a character."

Weren't they all?

"I'm a product. One that sells."

He leaned back in his seat. "I think you're much more than that, Ronie."

Ronie. Not Ronyika.

She put her buds in her ears, her hands shaking.

Oh, no. For the first time, she considered that she might not want to win after all.

FIVE

"You know, bro, you had us totally off the map about this woman. I expected some sort of misbehaving teenager. Vonya is one of the nicest people I've ever met." Luke stood at the window, overlooking Friedrich Strasse. He had rolled his dress shirt up at the cuffs, his blond hair was a wreck—although he liked it messy—and he had a five-o'clock shadow that Chet would disapprove of.

In fact, he might disapprove of the entire operation. Brody could admit it felt hacked together, slipshod. Thankfully, no one really believed that Vonya was in any danger. Still, their techie, Artyom, in a pair of faded jeans and a T-shirt—the look of a man who stayed behind the scenes—was already monitoring the chat sites, as well as reviewing video coverage from tonight's event. They'd track faces and see who showed up more than once.

Outside, the rain had stopped, the street shiny and freshly scrubbed.

Brody liked Berlin—the grandeur of the Brandenburg Gate, the architecture of the Reichstag.

Even this hotel had its perks. So what if it was a

re-creation of a hotel built in 1907—it felt old, with its marble lobby, stained-glass domed ceiling and Art Noveau fountain. And the piano player in the lobby added a touch of class.

Thankfully, they'd arrived incognito, without Vonya to mock the high-society feel that extended to the rooms, attired in gold and caramel and deep indigo blue. A cityscape picture hung over the double-long caramel sofa in the main living area. Sleek black-leather chairs surrounded a glass-and-metal coffee table, a flat-screen topped a dark walnut console, and in the adjoining room were two queen beds that he hadn't used nearly enough.

Brody would have preferred the penthouse for the entire crew, with its adjoining rooms and suite, but Ronie nixed that right off. Instead he'd reserved them suites on one end of the hall—his team's right across from Vonya and Leah.

"This is the nice Vonya. I'm not sure where the other one went," Brody said to Luke's assessment. He closed his cell phone. Hopefully the guy on the other end understood "pepperoni and mushroom." His German was so rusty, especially compared to Ronie's, that he might have just ordered schnitzel on his deep-dish pizza.

"I love her music." Artyom raised his voice from the adjoining room suite.

"You wouldn't know music if it hit you over the head, Russki. I've seen your version of entertainment in Moscow. If a disco ball isn't involved, it doesn't count."

"Tchaikovsky. Rachmaninoff. Need I say more?"

"Right. Like you've ever even heard them. And Vonya's a far cry from the classics."

But, okay, sure, he'd tapped his foot a few times tonight at her show. Even found himself smiling. Especially since the gig had gone off without a hitch.

He'd counted no less than seventeen wardrobe changes. She had the speed of a supermodel, and frankly, the woman must work out, because the trapeze act, which turned out to be a hit, was nothing less than acrobatic. The pyrotechnics show had him hoping her purple wig was fireproof.

All in all, it was success. No doubt everyone left a Vonya concert feeling happy. He'd finally figured out her product...happiness. Escape.

It really wasn't about music at all.

Although, he had to admit again, she could sing. What might her real voice, the one behind the mask, sound like?

Maybe sweet, like her laughter. Like yesterday, when Lyle had trounced her in chess. Although a big part of Brody suspected that perhaps she'd had to work hard to lose. Brody watched her—those eyes, which had layers of green and gold, lit right up, her laughter bright against the rainy pallor of the day.

"She might not be a classic but she has something special about her." Luke turned away from the window and lay down on the bed still, perhaps favoring his leg after last fall's gunshot wound. "I need some shut-eye. And, frankly, Wick, so do you. Vonya's tucked into bed for the night, her door locked, bars on the windows. You need some shut-eye."

"Actually, I thought I'd see if she'd like some pizza."

He heard the strange hope in his voice even as the words trundled out. Uh-oh.

Luke heard it, too. He looked over at him, eyebrow up. "You're bringing her…pizza?"

"Listen, she's been on her best behavior all week. Even cooperating." She texted him a picture of herself in her daily disguise in the mornings—see, wasn't that helpful? And she hung back and let him lead the way when they went out in public, in and out of transports, to the studio and back. The German paparazzi had tracked her down, but so far, all she'd done was wave. Not one move that might add a headline to their trip.

He had tried to reward her with silly gifts like making a latte run to Starbucks and meeting her in the lobby yesterday with a chocolate-filled kringle. So shoot him— they had looked delicious in the bakery case.

Nearly as delicious as her surprise when he'd handed her the bag at her door.

"Do I sense romance in the air? Because, you know, you're still on the job."

Brody held up his hand, like a shield against Luke's sentence. "No. I'm not that stupid. She's a client, and my job is to watch her back. I just…well, maybe I over-reacted. Maybe I did have her pegged wrong. Maybe she's not going to be any trouble after all."

"Uh, is that you letting your guard down, buddy? Because—"

"Listen, she's got a lot of baggage. Her sister died a few years ago after Vonya donated her kidney to her. That has to be tough, right?"

Luke said nothing.

"And her father is a real piece of work. Has the

emotions of a piece of ledgerock. I have a feeling no one in their family has ever dealt with their grief."

Artyom came and stood in the door, leaning his shoulder against the frame.

"I can't shake the feeling that there's more to her, and of course, I thought it meant she was up to something. Now I think she's just trying to survive. And if she has to do it in costume…"

He went over to the window, staring down at Luke's view.

"People do what they have to in order to survive."

Luke sat up. "Sounds like she's pretty hard on herself, if you ask me. Like she's blaming herself for her sister's death."

"Why would she blame herself? She had no control over her sister's body."

"It was her kidney. She has to feel responsible. Maybe she just can't forgive herself."

Yes, he understood not being able to forgive yourself.

You don't even like me. Why did her words keep coming back at him? Especially since, in fact, he *had* begun to like her—a little bit more every day.

Yes, the real Ronie had a startling sweetness. He saw it in the way she bantered with Lyle, and encouraged her band, and even kidded with Tommy D. In fact, Brody had started to suspect that perhaps there was something between them.

Not that it bothered him or anything, but what on this green planet would she see in Tommy D?

"You don't like him?"

Oh, good grief, had he been mumbling again? He closed one eye in a wince at Luke's question.

"He's just...pushy. He picks all Vonya's songs—especially the sexy ones. I saw her old stuff on You-Tube—she used to have a sweetness about her. Now during some of her songs, I feel like I should troll the crowd for stalkers."

"Feeling overprotective, Wick?"

"Here's a word for you, pal—*bodyguard*. Not that it's my favorite, but hey, it's what I'm getting *paid for*."

Luke smiled and picked up the remote. "Let's see if we can find something in English."

Brody leaned his forehead against the cool window. Overprotective. Maybe. Okay, so he was fond of Ronie, but only because he understood wanting to shake off the past but not knowing how to do it.

On the street, he saw a pizza delivery vehicle pull up.

"I'll be back." He grabbed the door key and headed down to the lobby.

The pizza man, not unlike the variety on the other side of the pond, haggled with the concierge. "That's for me," Brody said. He paid for the pizza at the desk, tipped the driver in euros and hit the button for the elevator.

Yes, he understood Ronie, finally. Something had broken open between them on the plane. He might even call it...trust.

The elevator opened. He let pass a woman in a metallic gray dress with black hair bobbed to her ears and bug sunglasses. Some sort of German starlet incognito, probably. Apparently, the hotel also housed other national highbrows—a billionaire from Greece, an Italian designer with his own slew of models, an African diplomat. He'd gotten the rundown from the security chief at the hotel.

He pushed the button for the fourth floor.

The pizza practically called to him to snag a piece of pepperoni. This was what international living did—made you crazy for home. Sure, he liked a good bratwurst or schnitzel now and then, but after the week he'd had, nothing but comfort food would make him sleep.

And now that Ronie was locked safely in her room, he just might do that.

But first, he'd see if she wanted a piece. Just because they were friends.

He stood outside her door for nearly a minute, letting his courage talk him into knocking. Friends. He was simply working the charm factor. Two Americans enjoying a large, deep-dish, pepperoni pizza.

He balanced the pizza box in one hand and knocked.

Leah cracked open the door. "Hey, Brody. What's up?"

"I brought a late-night snack. I was thinking that—"

The look on her face stopped him cold. Some people could lie. Some couldn't. And Leah clearly was in the second category. He could see her trying to conjure up a story, and fast.

"Where is she?" He put his hand on the door and pushed.

"Brody, no," she said even as she stepped aside, probably more from fear than acquiescence. "Listen, I tried to talk her out of it but she said she had to go."

Brody tossed the pizza onto the glass coffee table.

He stalked in to one bedroom, then in to the other. Lyle looked up at Brody. "Did you say pizza?"

Brody rounded on Leah. "Go where?" His voice lowered to barely a whisper.

Leah wrapped her arms around her waist and drew in a breath. "She'll be fine, Brody. She does this all the time. And I promise, no one will recognize her. She's in costume."

"Of course she is." He wanted to put his fist through a wall as he remembered the dark-haired starlet exiting the lift. "Black wig, a gray dress?"

Leah nodded.

"Where was she going?"

Leah made a face. "Do you promise not to be mad?"

"Leah, I am so beyond mad right now, but the truth is, this isn't about mad. It's about crazy. And me trying to keep her from getting hurt. *Please.*"

"She's at a party. For General Mubar's son."

Ronie had recognized the genius of Vonya the very first night she'd donned the dress, the wig and the mask and crept onto the stage over five years ago.

She could go anywhere and do anything, and no one would be the wiser. Even Brody, who she'd passed without him even blinking at her as she snuck past him on the way to the penthouse elevator.

She might even explain her actions away, blaming them on Vonya. Tell herself that she, Ronie or Veronica S. Wagner had nothing to do with the flamboyant character who seemed so far from the person she thought she was.

Vonya had sometimes gotten out of control, turning into someone even Ronie couldn't justify.

But tonight, for Kafara, Vonya would be her salvation.

She approached the door and handed the thug—a bald German the size of a linebacker—her invitation. He scanned the bar code. "You're Vonya?"

"In the flesh, baby." She puckered her bloodred lips at him and gave him an air kiss. He moved aside to let her enter the penthouse suite.

How convenient that Brody had picked this hotel for their accommodations, although why he'd had to find the most expensive hotel in Berlin was beyond her, unless… For a long, bone-chilling moment, she suspected he had figured her out.

But how could he know that she'd been using her Vonya persona as a cover ever since Zimbala, to ferry information as well as national secrets in and out of Europe as a CIA asset?

Yes, she kept that one close to her chest.

Not that she was on the payroll or anything. She just… well, she'd made friends with Clive Bishop, agent on the ground in Zimbala, and he'd needed a courier.

One time had turned into many.

Perhaps she did have a morsel of superspy in her because, yes, she loved the danger of knowing she carried highly sensitive, internal secrets across the ocean. Like footage of General Mubar's recruiting techniques. And the mass grave Bishop had uncovered, proving the genocide of thousands of innocent women and children.

But this gig was personal. Or, at least, once she finished her mission, it would be.

She moved into the huge array of rooms, a smile on her face as she picked up a glass of champagne for show and sashayed through the crowd. A techno-European mix of punk rock thumped out of giant speakers. The balcony door hung open, probably to offset the heat of so many bodies breaking the fire code. The television blared a soccer match. She recognized faces from tabloids—an Italian actress who would probably know her in pink hair, and a punk rocker she'd met at a Berlin club during her tour a year ago. None of them recognized her.

Thankfully. Because circulating around the room like piranha were a few invited paparazzi. Yeah, that'd be perfect—get her picture taken so her father could totally lose his mind over her "behavior."

And she didn't tell Tommy D, either. Last time she'd hung out with Damu Mubar, tabloid pictures had put them together as a couple and Tommy had practically come unglued. She didn't agree with her father that General Mubar knew her real identity. Damu had never suggested he knew her as anyone but Vonya. Still, she'd stay out of the press, just in case.

Not that Brody would be any better at holding it together if he found out. He'd be furious if he figured out she'd slipped out of her room—although she'd caught a whiff of that pizza and nearly turned around to chase after him.

But Damu Mubar's birthday came only once a year. And she hadn't cultivated a flirtatious friendship with the man just to derail it for a deep-dish pizza.

Oh, it probably had mushrooms…

And lots of sticky cheese…

She stopped a waiter, grabbing a sushi roll. Brody was probably holed up in his room, enjoying his pizza with the two other gorillas.

Okay, that wasn't fair. She did like Luke. And Artyom.

And after today, she would be on her best behavior. It was only tonight that she'd be trouble. She'd snuggle up to Damu, grab his cell phone, swipe the V-chip, copy it in the cute little device Bishop had left in her welcome basket, and then return it.

Transmit to Bishop and he'd do the rest.

See, nothing to get ruffled about, Brody.

And she didn't know why he had to get so uptight about her attire. She saw less clothing on the women here than on some remote islands in Indonesia. One woman walked by in what looked like two napkins and a placemat. Another wore a leopard-print scarf wound round and round her skinny frame.

She raised her glass to a Vonya look-alike—white wig, policeman's hat. Although she would never wear those strips of leather that doubled as a dress. Sorry, but she liked more material than that. Even her wings came with a blue, full-bodied leotard under it.

With everything inside her, she longed to be back in her suite, playing Mario with Lyle or reading the end of *Pride and Prejudice*. Or even watching Leah blog about their day on VonWatch.

Or enjoying a pizza with—

Stop. He wasn't her friend. Even if he thought he was.

There. Standing on the balcony, chatting up a shapely

blond. Damu Mubar had no problem making it as a tab-loid favorite thanks to his creamy dark skin, the charis-ma of his smile, the gym-honed frame and the millions of dollars he wore in his silk suits, his Italian shoes, the diamonds on his fingers.

The only son of General Mubar, Damu had reached out to Vonya during her first tour to Zimbala three years ago, when he graciously offered to be her tour guide and then led her expertly away from his father's child-soldier training camps and his more vocal dissenters. She'd picked up more quickly than the rest of the world that Mubar's "rescue" of the oppressed just meant turn-ing his guns on those who opposed him.

But for Bishop's and Kafara's sakes, she'd kept her mouth shut.

She slipped out onto the balcony. "Damu, you aren't boring this poor girl with your car collection, are you?" She looked at the blonde, who couldn't have been a day over eighteen, and winked.

Damu turned, a smile already shining as he held out his arms. Vonya slipped into his embrace. "My friend, Vonya. I'm so glad you came. And looking…yourself, as usual." He kissed her cheek, his chuckle low.

The blonde gave her a pout and headed back inside.

"I've missed you, Damu."

"I knew you couldn't stay away from me."

"I hope you saved me a dance." She ran her finger around her champagne glass. Yes, she'd felt his cell phone, a small rectangle in his jacket pocket, right side. Bingo.

He took her champagne, set it on the tray and took her hand.

A wooden dance floor had been set up in the center of the room, where she saw all manner of gyrations that passed for dancing. She took the floor, thankful for the dark lights and for the lessons Bishop had taught her in lifting a man's wallet—or in this case, cell phone. She danced around him, measuring the music, letting her hands find his arms, his waist, and then snake into his pocket to lift it out.

She palmed it into the sleeve of her dress, keeping her hands lifted, then twining them around him and pressing a kiss to the well of his sweaty neck. Ew. But she'd do it for Kafara.

For freedom.

For the information locked in Damu's cell phone.

"I'll be back," she said, and swayed a little, just for effect. Damu patted her backside as she twirled off the dance floor.

She sneaked into a bathroom off one of the bedroom suites, the pulse of the night slipping under the door, banging against the tiles. Or maybe it was her heartbeat. She'd done it. She shook the phone from her sleeve.

Oh, no. Not a phone—a microcomputer. She turned it on and a password prompt filled the screen.

No. She needed the phone. With the V-chip. Only the phone had the contact information of the man Damu planned to slip diamonds to on their final leg of the journey to America—diamonds that Damu had smuggled out of Zimbala. Agent Bishop and his team needed the contact info to intercept the shipment and shut down Mubar's money flow.

And Ronie needed to complete the mission in order

to keep her end of the deal with Bishop—a deal that ended with Kafara being rescued from Mubar's army.

She turned and stared at herself in the mirror. Sooty-black hair, bloodred lips, and fear in her eyes. She had to go back out there, slip the computer back into Damu's pocket, and find his cell phone.

Her hands shook as she slipped the phone back into her sleeve.

She took a breath.

Opened the door.

And wouldn't you know it, there stood the Boy Scout on the other side.

"Gotcha," Brody said, without a hint of a grin on his face.

SIX

Of course she'd run to Damu Mubar's birthday party. Because of all the places Ronie could run off to—a disco, a concert, even a late-night sushi place, the den of Damu Mubar, the son of the man who had threatened to kill her, seemed the most crazy.

Apparently, Miss Schizophrenia was back.

"This is off the charts, even for you, Ronie." He blocked her exit from the bathroom, even as she tried to step around him.

Yep, he now recognized the starlet from the elevator and wanted to throttle her—or himself, perhaps—for not seeing right through her "I'm so tired, I just need a good night's sleep" routine.

"Get out of my way." She stared up at him and for a second, fear flashed into her eyes. Wait—was she afraid of him?

No, there was something else, too. She held herself strangely, her arms around her waist. "What are you hiding?"

Again fear, covered fast by anger. "Nothing. Except not wanting to be antagonized by my bodyguard. I told you to stay out of my way."

"No, you told me you were going to bed. You lied to me."

A muscle pulsed in her throat as if his words actually hurt her. She again tried to step past him, but he backed her into the bathroom and shut the door.

She moved backward into the shower, her eyes wide.

"Oh, calm down. I'm not going to hurt you." He winced even as he said it—didn't she know him well enough by now?

Apparently not well enough to trust him. She still had her arms wrapped around herself. "What's going on? What are you doing here?" He tried to keep his voice low. It came out more wolf than whisper.

"I—I—Damu is a friend. He invited me."

"He's the son of the man who wants your father dead. Didn't you think, for one second, that this might be a trap? That he's been using your friendship to bait you? C'mon, Vonya, be smarter than that. Or aren't you?"

She flinched. "You…can't talk to me that way. You… you're *fired*."

Her words lacked in oomph, but the hatred in her eyes made up for it.

Well, so be it. They weren't supposed to be friends, anyway, and he'd been only fooling himself by letting down his guard.

Wow, was he an idiot.

"You can't fire me. That's the point. Now, we're leaving."

Outside, the music pulsed, the beat loud. He'd been nearly frantic when he arrived at the penthouse door, probably something that worked in his favor in convincing Mubar's bouncer to let him in. Trying to find Vonya in the mass of humanity out there—well, it was a good thing he'd seen her on the dance floor.

With Damu.

Which nearly made him lose his mind.

"Get out of my way." She came at him again.

"Not on your life, Party Girl. You're leaving. Now. With me."

That set her jaw on edge. She narrowed her eyes at him. And for the first time since he'd stopped her at the threshold, she seemed to stop trembling.

"Brody, I know you won't understand this, but I have to stay and dance with Damu. It's…important. I promise, I'm not in any danger." She took a breath. "Please?"

Really? She thought he'd fall for that? He couldn't help it—a chuckle escaped. "Wow, you're good. I nearly bought that. But…uh…no. What kind of woman walks right into danger?" She opened her mouth but he held up his hand. "The kind who needs her head examined. Party's over, honey. Don't make me carry you out of here."

Her eyes widened at that. "Brody—please."

And right then, he was back in a hot, dusty desert, the dirt kicking up around Shelby as she said, *"Brody— please!"*

No, no, *no,* he wasn't going back there, wasn't going to let some woman led by her emotions run into her own death and drag him along with her so she could die in his shaking arms.

No, no, *no.*

What was it with him attracting women who didn't

mind looking death in the eye and shaking their fists at it?

"I'm not leaving," she said, in a voice that might break another man.

Not him. "If that's how you want it."

He didn't spare her dignity when he advanced on her, picked her up and threw her over his shoulder. She slammed her fist into his spine, a solid blow that might have buckled him if he hadn't been powering on sheer fury.

He opened the bathroom door, let her kick, and then decided on prudence.

Walking through the party with Vonya over his shoulder just might be a surefire way to end up in the tabloids.

"Promise to come nicely."

"Put me down."

"Von—"

She kicked again—wow, she was strong. Clearly she wasn't going to cooperate.

Fine.

"Make a hole!" He charged out of the bathroom and then the bedroom, hand out, not caring who he banged into, not caring that she was beating his back as he went. Not caring about the stares he got, or even some laughter from those who recognized, well, probably her backside. Which, really, he apologized for inside, even if she'd never know it.

He marched her past Damu, who looked up from the blonde he was dancing with and even came toward them. Brody held up a hand in warning and Damu's eyes flashed.

Brody guessed he had about ten seconds before this thing went south.

He aimed straight for the door and blew right past the bouncer, who gave him a raised eyebrow and a smirk.

Not that kind of party, dude. Brody wanted to put his fist into the guy's face.

He set Vonya down right outside the elevator, steadying her on those high heels. And proving that they'd advanced oh-so-far in their relationship, she reached back and let loose with a bone-jarring slap.

And once again, as the elevator door opened, the paparazzi managed to catch it all in a blinding flash of white light.

In the stone-cold silence between them in the elevator, Ronie realized something had died.

The only word she could put to it might be... *friendship.*

She hated that she cared. That she'd actually looked forward to the morning macchiatos. The chocolate pastries. Seeing his dark eyes on her during rehearsal. Measuring. Protecting.

She hated the fact that she liked it—all of it.

For a second, seeing the anger in Brody's eyes, her throat burned, and she'd wanted to rewind back to the moment when she opened the bathroom door and saw him standing there.

Like he'd come after her. To rescue her. And in a crazy moment, she'd wanted to—

"What were you thinking?" he said.

She folded her arms and set her jaw. *I was thinking about saving someone's life,* she wanted to say.

"Did you not care that you might get, oh, I don't know, killed?"

"Damu wouldn't hurt me. We're friends."

"Apparently you don't know the meaning of the word."

Ouch. She nearly leaped through the doors as they opened. She stalked back to her room and knocked on the door.

He inserted the key into the lock for her. She pushed through and turned to slam the door, but of course he charged in, caught the door, and shut it behind him with a soft click.

Leah looked up from where she was working on her computer at the glass table. Lyle's door was closed, light pulsing from it, evidence of a television on in a dark room.

"Get out," Vonya snarled.

"You've got to be kidding me," he said softly.

Leah closed her laptop. "I'll see you in the morning." She eyed Brody and shook her head before closing the bedroom door behind her. Perfect.

"I'm fine now, you can go."

"So you can leave again? I'm done trying to figure you out, or even trust you, Ronie. Congratulations, you have a new roommate." He turned, threw the dead bolt on the door, then walked over and sat on the sofa.

Seriously? "Listen, Brody, okay. I'll stay here." The lie slipped through her teeth, tasting sour even to herself. "I've learned my lesson."

His explosion of laughter rocked her back. "Okay, darlin'. What was I thinking? Of course you will." He walked over to the closet, opened it and grabbed the extra pillow from the shelf. Then he tossed it down in front of the door. "I think I'll just sleep right here if it's all the same to you."

She stared at him, at his set jaw, his dark eyes.

"Oh, of all the overreactions. Fine. Suit yourself."

Her room had a door, too. She marched into her bedroom, turned on the light and locked the door behind her. Then she went to the outside door and flung it open.

"Going somewhere?" Luke turned and smiled, his arms folded against his chest.

"Just down the hall for some ice."

Luke looked at her empty hands.

"Fine!" She slammed the door, turned and sank down against it. Nice. Perfect.

She'd stolen Damu's computer. And when he found it missing, it wouldn't take him long to figure out who had taken it. Which meant that General Mubar would discover someone was onto him and send the smuggler deeper into hiding.

She'd never get Kafara out of the Zimbalan army.

Stupid hot wig. She yanked it off, threw it across the room and ran her fingers through her short, mousy hair. Then she pulled the computer out of her sleeve and turned it on.

That same annoying password prompt lit up the screen. She tried *Damu*. Incorrect. *Mubar*. Incorrect.

She stared at it, shaking it in her hands. "Why?"

"Are you okay in there?" came Brody's hard voice.

"Leave me alone."

"Not on your life."

She wanted to hurl the computer at him, but, well,

that wouldn't quite get it working, would it? But she was itching for something—someone—to hurt.

This much of her father, yes, she had in her.

Instead she climbed to her feet, set the computer on the bureau.

She walked to the window, staring down onto the street. Bright lights shone on the Brandenburg Gate, underlighting the Quadriga on top, the four horses drawing a chariot as if emerging from battle. She still found it hard to believe that this city had once lain in rubble. That even this hotel had been nothing but stones and rebar before they'd rebuilt it to its original grandeur. She wanted to linger every time they passed through the lobby and listen to the pianist, maybe belly up to the piano herself and plunk out a tune.

There had to be a way to figure out how to get into that computer.

Leah might know—she acted as her computer guru. Or even Lyle. The kid seemed to know how to make her cell phone do things she never dreamed it could do.

No, she needed a serious techie.

What about Artyom? Okay, her synapses simply weren't functioning. She needed someone who wouldn't shut her down—like one of Bishop's contacts.

She dug her phone out of her bag and texted him.

The CIA couldn't kill her if she was trying to solve her problem, right?

She waited a moment and when no reply came she went into the bathroom and turned on the shower.

She always did prefer to do her crying in the bathroom.

She scrubbed off the black eyeliner, the red lips, the

pasty makeup. Soon, plain old Ronie stared back at her in the mirror, those unimpressive eyes now bloodshot. And, of course, now she was hungry. Which meant she'd have to order room service, when what she really wanted was that pizza.

But she'd die of starvation before she'd ask Brody for a piece.

But how had he found out she was missing? She'd only conjured up the plan after a week of behaving exactly how she had tonight—wishing him good-night and going to her room. He never came to check on her, never camped out in the hall.

He'd trusted her.

And she'd betrayed him. Doubly betrayed him, because it came to her then that he'd probably come to the door…with the pizza. After all, he'd been delivering all sorts of goodies to her all week. Like they might really be friends.

No wonder he came charging into the party with both barrels loaded.

And that accounted for why he'd looked wounded when she opened the door and nearly plowed into him.

And yes, seeing him that angry had shaken her.

Because ever since the plane, well…something about him made her think she wasn't alone. She'd given him a part of herself and he hadn't wasted it.

He actually made her feel as though someone actually…*saw* her.

Or at least was trying to. And what would that be like, really? To have someone look beyond Vonya, or even Veronica, to see the real Ronie? Truthfully, did she even know that girl? She'd died, perhaps, right alongside Savannah.

Along with her sense of self-preservation.

What kind of woman walks right into danger?

No. she refused to believe Damu meant her harm. He was just a playboy, spending his daddy's money. Besides, Bishop would warn her if she was in real danger.

A knock at her door. She stiffened, checked her face, then took a breath and opened the door.

Leah stood in her pajamas and bathrobe. "Can I come in?"

Ronie hauled her into the room and wrapped her arms around her.

Leah unwound Ronie's arms from her. "I tried to lie, but he saw right through me. And…well, he's sort of intimidating."

"What did he do to you to make you tell?" She saw his face the second before he tossed her over his shoulder.

"Nothing." Leah winced. "I admit, I was worried about you, too. So…I caved." She flopped onto the bed. "I'd make a horrible spy. I'm so sorry."

"Shh. He has his minions parked everywhere." She pointed at the door to the hallway.

Leah clamped her hand over her mouth. "Sorry. So did you get it?"

Ronie lifted the computer from the bureau. "Not exactly. It's a computer—one of those PDAs with toys on it. It's protected by a password."

"Do you think it has the information you need on it?"

"I don't know. Maybe. But Brody the Boy Scout

hauled me out of the party before I could put it back and get the cell phone."

Leah raised an eyebrow. "Hauled you out?"

"Over his shoulder. Like a fireman. Stop smiling."

Leah picked up a pillow and sank her face into it.

Ronie shook her head. "Perfect. And you'll be overjoyed to know that the paparazzi got a picture of it. Probably a nice shot of my backside."

"It's not such a bad backside, you know."

"Please stop."

"Well, it's nice to know that if you needed him, Brody would appear."

"Oh, there's not a doubt in my mind he'd break down doors for me. Like some sort of knight in shining armor. Except, well, I'm not sure if you noticed but I'm not a girl who needs heroes. I can rescue myself, thank you very much. Have, in fact, too many times to count."

Like that moment in D.C., when she'd been cowering behind the speaker, hurt and very, very afraid? She'd needed a hero then, hadn't she?

And, yes, every time she dangled from the trapeze swing, she nearly got rope burns, her hands growing slick. Seeing Brody staring up at her made her feel, oddly, safe.

Even tonight, when she'd opened the door and seen him standing there, a dark wall of power, okay, she'd gone a little weak.

She'd wanted to throw herself into his arms.

She actually saw herself doing it, too. Because for a week now, she'd wondered what it might feel like to have his arms close around her for real. To breathe in that spicy, male smell.

To know what was behind those intense dark eyes. To get beyond the strange game they were playing to the real Brody. She wanted to hear his secrets and make him feel everything she felt with him.

Safe.

Understood.

Friends, or…more.

Apparently you don't know the meaning of the word.

Oh, no, she'd have to get back into the shower.

"You like him, don't you?"

Ronie lifted a shoulder.

"You know, you're not dishonoring your sister by falling in love, Rons. I think Savannah would approve."

Ronie winced. "I'm not, it's not, I mean—"

"Stop. You've been dodging romance for as long as I've known you, and I can only believe it's because you think you don't deserve it."

Maybe she should just live in the shower. "I…deserve it."

"Say it again like you actually mean it." Leah threw the pillow at her.

Ronie caught it. "I just don't have time. I'm busy."

"Saving the children of the world. Sure. But here's the strange part. I have this feeling that if Brody knew what you were doing, he might actually be on your side."

"I doubt that, Leah."

"You could try telling him."

"Right. He'd never leave my side."

"And that's a bad thing because…?"

Ronie threw back the pillow. "Listen. Brody isn't interested in me, I can guarantee it. Especially after tonight. If he was disgusted with me before, I promise you, he can't stand me now."

"He's outside in the living room. Is that the mark of a man repulsed?"

"It's the mark of a man well paid. The thing is, I can do this. I know it. I just need some wiggle room. And now Brody won't let me go ten feet away from him."

Leah nodded at her words. "And again, why is that a bad thing?"

"Whose side are you on here, Leah?"

Leah slid off the bed, came over and took Ronie's hands. "Yours, friend. Always yours." She gave Ronie a hug. "Get some sleep."

"I'm hungry, actually."

"I think there's some food in the fridge. But that would require you to, you know, confront the Beast by the Castle Door," She winked as she slipped out.

I think Savannah would approve.

Yes, she probably would. He did look a lot like the heroes of their daydreams.

Stop. She didn't have room in her life for daydreams. Not when Kafara lived in his own private nightmare.

It had nothing to do with deserving anything.

She wiped her eyes, padded over to the door and opened it.

Brody sat with his back to the hallway door, eyes closed. He opened them, though, when he heard her and raised an eyebrow. "Where's Vonya?"

"Funny."

She padded out and opened the fridge in the suite. Yes, thank you, someone had put the fruit bowl in the fridge. She pulled out an orange.

"You're not planning on throwing that at me, are you?"

She looked at the orange. "I probably deserved that."

His eyes gentled and it worked a lump into her throat. "You know, I'm just trying to do my job here."

She took a breath and pulled her bathrobe around her in a tight fist at her neck. "I'm sorry, Brody. I… It won't happen again."

"You bet it won't, because as of right now, Mr. Nice Guy is gone."

She nodded. "Good night." She slipped back into her room and put the pillow over her head. Unfortunately, a big part of her had begun to really like Mr. Nice Guy. She would miss him—a lot.

SEVEN

The air bore the smell of rotten meat, a barrel fire, the decay of mud huts. She spotted Kafara even before the Jeep stopped and waved to him.

But he had his back to her, chopping soapstone with a machete. A giant pile of rough-hewn sandstone towered over him like a pyramid.

"Kafara!"

He didn't turn, just kept chopping.

Around him, other boys with their rusty machetes hacked the stone. She got out, her feet bare on the dry earth. It dusted her ankles and her legs. "Kafara!"

He turned then, smiling at her, his teeth white against his black face. "Miss Vonya!"

The woman appeared. She always seemed to come from nowhere, although deep in Ronie's subconscious she knew she must live in the village. She carried a burlap bag on her head, tied neatly, balanced on a coil of rope. As Kafara ran close, she dropped the burlap and let it open.

A pineapple rolled out.

Kafara picked it up. "You want one?" he asked Vonya.

She always said yes, even though she could practically hear herself moan, *No. No.*

Kafara held the pineapple in his hand. He chopped off the top, then the bottom. Then, balancing it in his hands, he brought his machete down through the bulk of it.

Blood spurted out, spraying them, coating Vonya.

She screamed, shaking herself out of her dream, sweat coating her. "Stop! Stop!"

The door banged open and a beast roared into the room.

"What is it?"

She looked up and saw a man holding a spatula in one hand, a gun in the other. He looked rabid enough to shoot.

"I—I—" She struggled to catch her breath, then fell back into the pillows. She stared at the creamy white ceiling and listened to the traffic outside.

Berlin. She was in Berlin and—

"Are you okay?"

Brody. She pulled the sheet over her, having clearly wrestled and lost to the bed linens. He turned, checked the closet, the bathroom. Then he holstered his gun—how long had he had that?—and came back to the bed. He stood over her with a strange mix of horror and anger on his face.

"I thought you were being ripped apart limb from limb in here."

"Are you okay, Rons?" Leah came into the room, wrapping her robe around her. "Another nightmare?" She sat down on the side of the bed and drew Ronie into her arms. "You're shaking."

She wanted to close her eyes but then Kafara would be there again, wouldn't he? So she stared up at Brody. He blew out a long breath.

"I'm fine." She drew away, meeting Leah's eyes. "I'll be fine, really. This is what happens when you eat an orange before going to bed. You dream about citrus fruits."

Brody frowned. Leah shook her head. "Not funny." She looked at Brody. "She has nightmares about a bleeding pineapple every once in a while."

He didn't look convinced. *And thank you, Leah, for leaving out the part about Kafara. And the machete. And the fact that it wasn't about a pineapple at all, was it?*

"Get up, and come eat. Turns out your bodyguard is also Chef Ramsey. He makes a mean omelet." Leah shooed Brody out of the room and closed the door behind them.

Ronie lay back into her pillow. Kafara. She just knew he was in trouble—he had to be. Life expectancy in General Mubar's army was less than a year.

Kafara had been in for nearly six months already.

A beep made her throw back the covers and grab her cell phone. She'd missed three messages.

The first had been sent an hour after she went to bed: *Msg received. Finding help.*

The next two arrived only five minutes ago. Maybe that was what triggered her dream.

Cmptr Hlp found. Prague.

And:

Next concert date?

She replied, then deleted the communication.

By the time she got out of the shower, a final message appeared. *Meet after concert, at Tyn Church. Old Towne Square.*

Old Towne Square, home of the famous Gothic church with the two black-roofed towers that reminded her of some Disney movie. She'd been there before—her concert venue happened to be only a few blocks away. Yes.

See? This didn't have to be a disaster.

She went to the window, watching traffic negotiate Friedrich Strasse. Yesterday's rain had turned the city sparkly and fresh. The oaks and maples were a crisp green, the geraniums deep red in their planters.

And the smell of eggs sizzling in butter nearly turned her inside out. She didn't bother with makeup—just pulled on her jeans and a T-shirt, took a breath, and forayed into the suite.

Indeed, Brody stood in the tiny makeshift kitchen cooking. He had little ramekins of onion, green pepper, mushrooms, cheese and bacon bits lined up on the counter, like some sort of short-order cook.

"What's this?"

Brody looked like he might smile, but he bit it back.

"There will be no more fancy eating in the main dining room, although I know how you love the kringle buffet. However you'll just have to settle for room service…or just ordinary me. Care for an omelet? I make a pretty mean one, even if it is only the basics."

Of course he did. What didn't he do well? "The works, please."

He raised an eyebrow but nodded. "As you wish."

Then he poured the egg batter in the hot pan. The omelet sizzled as it cooked.

"I didn't know omelets came with your services. It's not in the brochure."

He didn't look at her as he poured her a glass of juice, setting it before her. "There's a lot not listed in the brochure." He then let half the smile free. "Including a listening ear. But I'm pretty good at that if you want to air out your thoughts."

Oh, don't do this. Don't be nice. She considered his tousled dark hair and the fact that, yes, he appeared to have slept by her door, the big bulldog.

She'd have to keep her wits about her if she hoped to sneak away again. She picked up the paper, pretending to read the front page. She couldn't be friendly—he'd only see through that, even if she meant it. And if she were belligerent, he'd only get more suspicious.

She'd have to get creative. Somehow.

"Sorry about the picture on page eight."

She turned to it, and found her backside smack in the center of the page. Another shot featured her hand connecting with Brody's cheek. "I've seen the second one before."

"It seems to be our trademark."

She couldn't ignore the strange feeling that slipped through her at those words.

"Sorry about the other one, though," he said, slipping her omelet onto a plate. "I guess there's no hiding out now."

"What do you mean?"

"I'd hoped to keep you—and me—out of the tabloids." He handed her the plate, along with a napkin roll, a fork and knife tucked inside.

"Why?"

"Because then whoever might hurt you knows what I look like. They know I'm looking out for you. Generally, bodyguards like to stay under the radar."

"Oh. Sorry."

He turned back to the kitchen. "Vonya's not a real under-the-radar gal. I shouldn't have set my sights so high."

She wasn't sure why, but his words felt delivered up with sharp objects embedded in them. "I'll…I'll try to stay out of trouble."

He picked up an orange and tossed it in his hand. "Yep." Then he began to peel it.

She wasn't sure why his smugness made her want to hurl something at him, but if she had fruit of any kind nearby, she'd be aiming for his head.

Instead she took the paper, folded it and dropped it onto the floor. "I despise the tabloids. If I never saw another one again, I'd rejoice with singing and tambourines."

"And swinging," he said, in a voice so quiet he may have thought she wouldn't catch it.

"What, you don't like the swinging song?"

He finished peeling the orange and broke off a section. "It gives me a coronary. I just know you're going to fly off that swing and I'm not going to be able to catch you."

He would try to catch her?

"Is somebody making breakfast? I'm hungry." Lyle

appeared at the door, wearing his Halo pajama pants and a Hollister T-shirt.

"Good morning, Lyle," she said, picking up her fork to glare at Brody.

The twelve-year-old shuffled into the room, holding his Nintendo. He stopped at the table, his thumbs moving.

"Yes!" He looked up, grinning at Ronie. "I got to the next level."

"Good job." Oh, how she loved that smile. Just having him around, seeing him strong and healthy, made her want to cheer.

He walked up to Brody. "Hey, man, how you doing? Want to play a round of Mario Cart?"

She could have imagined it, but Brody stiffened, and then to her shock, a strange look crossed his face.

She'd almost call it fear.

"I don't play games, kid," he said, and turned away.

It suddenly hit her that maybe that had been the problem all along. He hadn't been playing games. He had offered her his hand—and macchiatos and pastries and even pizza—in friendship.

And she'd all but spit on it.

She stared at her omelet, spilling out vegetables, and took a bite. Simple, but delicious.

Maybe that was the key. She shouldn't have played games with him, either. She'd landed them in this mess, and now she'd have to be the one to sort it out. No, she didn't have to tell him everything, but what if she simply…was herself? While she'd blown any chance of Brody trusting her again, maybe they could be civil to each other. Maybe even become real friends.

She was just so tired of pretending, tired of the masks.

Of Vonya.

She took another bite. Yes, delicious. And simple.

No more games. At least not until Prague.

The woman just might drive him back over the ocean and straight into the loony bin.

Or at least, now that he was back in Prague, with his apartment only two blocks away, back to his own digs where he could get a decent night's sleep and perhaps figure out where he'd left his marbles.

"Who is this woman?" Brody said into his lapel mike. Luke stood on the other side of the room, watching the entrances and Brody's back.

"What, you've never seen a pop diva tie balloon animals before?"

"I just didn't know you could make so many different animals with balloons. Is that a monkey?"

He hadn't expected the woman the world knew as Vonya to sit in the middle of an orphanage in the Czech Republic and tie balloon animals for a group of four-year-olds.

And, wouldn't you know it, she was good at it, too. Dogs and elephants and birds and even hats. She laughed with the children and spoke to them in what sounded like half German and half Russian.

"What's that language she's speaking?" Luke asked.

"She calls it Czech-ish. Although, let's be clear here, it's not one of the four languages she speaks fluently. They happen to be German, Dutch, Russian and English.

And a smattering of Spanish, Italian and, well, Czech, apparently."

From across the room, Luke raised an eyebrow.

"You know what she told me this morning?" Brody continued. "That German, Russian and Czech are so similar, she can almost speak to half of eastern Europe. Which of course, she does."

"Sounds like you're learning a lot there, over on her sofa, pal. I don't suppose you want to switch places."

Brody glared at him.

No. Only he wasn't sure why, because clearly the woman was up to her games again. He just couldn't figure out the rules.

"Did you know she plays the guitar?" Acoustic, and she hummed as she did it. It stirred him in a way he couldn't voice, thrumming a place inside.

And she sang in the shower—not that he'd ever mention that. But her voice drifted out, as if she had no idea the walls seemed to be constructed of papier-mâché. And it was a husky, bluesy voice, too—not a hint of the pop diva when she was sudsing up, apparently.

She also liked apples with peanut butter on them. He'd found her sneaking little tubs of peanut butter as they passed the restaurant buffet, even though they were all eating in their rooms these days.

"I'll get you your own jar."

"No. This is more fun." She winked at him. "Besides, you'll be hard-pressed to find peanut butter in a European grocery store. It's an American thing."

And then there was the Nutella fascination. She ate it with a spoon. And on bread and crackers. And apples, of course. And even on her oatmeal.

How she fit into those little outfits was beyond him, except for the fact that she rehearsed like a maniac. All week she'd drummed the new cues into her band in anticipation of the weekend shows—two of them, at a venue not far from his apartment. She dropped into an exhausted heap on the sofa, or went to bed early, every night.

She'd turned into no-fun Ronie. Just what game did she have them playing now?

At least this Vonya seemed to be cooperating, which worked in their favor, because he couldn't shake the feeling of eyes on him as he followed her around Prague. As if, indeed, someone were watching them. "You sure you vetted everyone at the club? Because I can't shake a feeling that something is going to go south," Brody said to his team.

Artyom's voice came over the communication system. "Stop freaking out, Wick. Everything's fine."

Maybe it was the tabloid picture—it had of course circulated around the web, until finally it came back to him in the form of an untitled email with just a question mark from his boss, Chet.

Who, apparently, got online just fine from whatever Mediterranean beach he happened to be lounging on.

"I'd appreciate it if you'd pass that a-okay along to Chet," Brody said.

"Thanks, boss, but you're the chief when the boss is away. You get all the fun."

"What did you find out about Damu?"

"He's in Paris. Not at all headed this direction."

Since Ronie's screaming episode—a memory that still woke him in the night in a cold sweat—he'd done some studying up on Damu Mubar and his father. Apparently, General Mubar had been "elected" by the people after a bloody coup. Heralded as a champion of the impoverished, he "helped" the elite in Zimbala distribute their wealth to the masses.

Which, generally meant him taking over, via the use of the national army and the lucrative diamond mines, and overseeing the country's largest export.

But what did that have to do with Ronie's nightmare about…a pineapple?

It probably bothered him more than it should have. But he simply couldn't erase the image of the terror on her face, her unseeing eyes, the way she tore at her sheets. Yes, he wanted to turn that nightmare inside out.

Ronie said something to the children that made them laugh, then they piled on her. Well, she did look a little like Barney the Dinosaur in her purple wig and unitard. Thankfully, she wore a black tuxedo jacket over the entire outfit.

Really, he wanted to strangle whoever picked out her clothes. Probably Tommy the Delightful, who'd made Brody's life ever so fun every day of this trip. Almost as if his presence annoyed him, Tommy spoke to Brody only in short, clipped sentences. Had it been the multiple personality quip that day on the set?

And no, Brody wouldn't be bringing him coffee, thank you.

At least Leah liked Brody, even if her son drove him crazy.

He could admit Lyle was a nice kid, and clearly Ronie adored him, spending most of her free time playing chess with him. And he seemed polite, used his pleases and thank-yous and didn't interrupt. You didn't see that much anymore. But every time he walked into the room, he simply rubbed Brody's fur up. He hadn't noticed it before he moved onto the sofa, but suddenly everything Lyle did made him clench his teeth. Couldn't the kid tell one joke that was funny?

"Mr. Wickham?" There was that politeness again. "I need to use the rest—"

"Stick around, kid. She's nearly done. You can go when we get to rehearsal."

The boy turned away.

"Using your niceness again, Wick? You'd better tone it down or you're going to have a fan club," Luke said, disapproval in his tone.

"We're about to leave."

"Sheesh, Wick. Weren't you *ever* a kid?"

Brody watched, as Luke motioned to Lyle and directed him to the bathroom.

Perfect.

Ronie finished hugging the kids and waved as she swept past him into the hallway.

He caught up with her, settling his hand on the small of her back. "You were great in there."

"Uh, thank you." Surprise filled her eyes.

He led her down the steps. The countryside of the Czech Republic still bore the marks of the Communist regime. The mustard-yellow orphanage seemed well-groomed but weeds poked up through the cracked sidewalk, and rusty yard equipment evidenced a zero budget for repairs.

Ronie stopped Tommy as she reached the van he'd

rented for the day. "You gave the check to the director, right?"

"Of course."

"Okay. She didn't mention it, so…" She shrugged. "Not that she should." She patted Tommy's chest. "Thank you."

Brody made a mental note to have Artyom follow up.

They drove back into the city, the buildings morphing from rustic to slick and modern, to classic as they wound toward Old Town. They passed under the ancient Powder Gate, with its Gothic black-tiled roof, and Ronie turned strangely quiet.

"Are you okay?"

She lifted a shoulder. "I've been here three times, and I've never toured the city. It's so beautiful, but I always miss it."

"You've never toured the city? It's the most beautiful in Europe." He didn't mention that he lived just on the other side of the Charles Bridge, in the foothills below Prague Castle.

"I fly in, rehearse, do the show and leave. I've been all over Europe and have never even seen it."

"We need to fix that. Driver, take us back to the hotel. Ronie, you're going to spend the day as a tourist."

"Brody, I have to rehearse, I can't—"

He held up his hand. "Consider this protection from overwork. I've seen the show—over and over, actually—and it's awesome."

Was that a blush? Hard to tell, but she swallowed. "Really?"

He nodded. "Really, Ronie, you have it nailed." He

turned to Leah. "You think you and Lyle can find something to do tonight? I can point you to a pizza joint."

She winked at him. "We'll be fine."

Ronie's big eyes gazed at him, and for a second, an unfamiliar heat went through him, something quick and warm and sweet. He swallowed it away. "Listen, this is my town. Let me show it to you."

And when she smiled, the feeling returned.

That smile might be the most dangerous side of her that he'd seen yet.

EIGHT

"Have you ever had a pig's knuckle?" Brody stood in the sunshine outside their quaint hotel on the corner of Old Town Square, wearing a pair of dark glasses and looking exactly like a tourist.

Not that he'd ever fit into the category of mere tourist. Not with those cheekbones and that wry smile. Or his wind-combed hair, the way he filled out his green polo shirt, or the low-slung, faded jeans. And, just to be unpredictable, he wore a pair of black high-top Converse tennis shoes.

Yes, this just might be fun.

"What kind of question is that to ask a girl?" She pulled on her cap, her head feeling light and airy without a wig. She'd taken a quick shower to remove the feeling of Vonya from her skin, and her short hair took all of thirty seconds to dry. She hadn't even styled it—just ran some product through it. She'd thrown on some jeans, a T-shirt, Leah's Mary Jane Sketchers and hit the road.

She couldn't remember ever feeling so…irresponsible. A giddy, almost intoxicating wildness filled her, bubbling out in a smile as he turned.

"Simply a practical question. I don't want you dropping from hunger halfway through the day."

"Just try to keep up, pal."

He chuckled and she felt it deep inside her chest. It only stirred the giddy feeling inside.

The tall, black roof spires of the Tyn Cathedral rose from beyond the cobblestone square, and she half expected a dragon to appear over the top and level the onlookers below with its fiery breath.

On every side, three-story buildings like something out of a storybook, with their red-tiled roofs, gated the square. Some were adorned with the ornate scrolls and floral bouquets of the Renaissance facades, others with baroque cherubs, and still others with the rounded Art Nouveau styling. In the center, men spilling at his feet, stood a statue of some reformer.

Bistros pushed out into the expanse, the tables covered with bright umbrellas, hosting diners from all nations eating al fresco. Pigeons cooed in groups over the cobblestones, uneven and black. A driver in a top hat drove a prettied-up horse and carriage.

"It's enchanting."

"And old. Prague was founded in the ninth century. It's best known as the place that gave us good old St. Wenceslas."

"From the Christmas song?"

"One and the same. C'mon, I want to show you something." He reached out, and for some reason she let him take her hand and pull her across the grassy park toward the old town hall. "Can we see the big, scary cathedral?"

"Later."

"You promise?" It would certainly help to get a little lay of the land before tomorrow night's big event. But even as she thought it, she tasted a swell of shame. Not only did she have Damu's computer in her possession, but here Brody was, showing her his city, and she planned on using the information to betray him. Again.

Swell.

"I promise, you'll get to see the 'big, scary' church."

His hand felt warm and gentle around hers.

Probably just part of his protection duties. So he wouldn't lose her in the crowd.

Soon they were staring at a tall clock with two faces, with small figures guarding it. "This is the Astronomical Clock. At the top of the hour, it chimes, and all the apostles rotate through those open doors. Then the cock crows three times. The different figures represent things despised by the culture of the time—vanity, greed, death and infidelity. It's on the old Czech time scale, but it also calculates the positions of the sun and the moon, and keeps track of the seasons."

"It's brilliant."

"So much so that the king at the time, so legend goes, had the creator's eyes plucked out so he wouldn't create it for anyone else."

"Nice."

"Sort of puts a damper on creativity. But that's not what I wanted to show you." He took her hand again and tugged her through the crowd. They passed an outdoor seating area, long tables covered with checked umbrellas. She slowed at the sight of a plate piled high with seafood linguine.

"Keep moving, Wonder Girl. I'll feed you, I promise. It's part of my job."

She could embrace that part of his job. They wandered under a gateway between streets, then emerged into a narrow, cobblestone alleyway. Golden buildings hovered over them, centuries of architecture in the moldings around the windows, the ornate carvings over the doors.

"Back in the day, houses were known for their emblems. A person might rent a room at the House of the Red Sheep. Or a tavern might be the House of the Golden Well. And of course, there are stories behind each emblem."

They passed a nook where a baker poured pancake mix onto a hot griddle. The thin blini bubbled up and he flipped it with a long wooden paddle. Ronie stopped, ignoring Brody's prodding, when she saw the man scoop out Nutella and smear it on the blini before rolling it up and dusting it with powdered sugar. "Oh, I must have one of those." She dug into her pocket. "Oh, no, I left my money in my room."

"You don't need it."

Why not? Was this…a date?

"Thanks, but I'll pay you back."

His lips tightened. "You could let someone do something nice for you, you know." He handed a bill to the man behind the counter.

She said nothing. No, actually, she couldn't. She took the treat wrapped in wax paper and bit into the pancake, letting the hazelnut chocolate dissolve in her mouth. "I could die right here, right now."

"Please don't say that to someone employed to keep you alive."

She laughed. "Now I just need something to drink."

"Demanding." He guided her toward another alley. "Welcome home."

Starbucks. She wanted to break into a run. "How—"

"Oh, all of Prague revolted when Starbucks moved in, but there are about five in the city now."

She entered the store and ordered a macchiato. Brody held her coffee as she finished off the blini. Then she took the coffee, following him back out to the street.

"Where to next?"

"Now that you've visited the most important site in Prague, how about we stop by Prague Castle, by way of the Charles Bridge?"

"You're hilarious." She followed him through another set of winding alleys, past tiny stores set in the nooks and crannies of ancient buildings. She stopped at a display of scarves, looking at a red one. She smiled up at him as she looped the scarf around her neck. "Put it on my tab."

"No tab. My treat, and don't argue. That looks nice on you."

His words caught her breath. It did?

"Let's detour." He reached out to take her hand again, and she debated a second before letting him. Well, she had to let the man do his job.

He led her through a walled archway into a lush garden. The street noise slipped away, and quiet ruled the courtyard, broken only by the trickle of water. He led her to a bench. Across from them a giant tree filled with hanging roses freshened the air.

"It's called Klementinum. It's a monastery."

"It's so peaceful."

"I come here sometimes. When I need to think. Or read my Bible."

His *Bible?* When was the last time she'd met someone who read their Bible? Maybe, well, never.

Once upon a time she'd read it, but her Bible had only become a reminder of how far she'd fallen.

Or maybe where she'd never been in the first place.

"How long have you lived here?"

"About a year, since I joined Stryker International."

"You like your job?"

He lifted a shoulder. "Sometimes." He stood, then held out his hand to pull her up.

Like now? For a wild second, she wanted to be one of the "sometimes."

They walked through another entrance to the monastery and came out onto a busy alleyway filled with more vendors.

"C'mon, Shop Girl. Let's see the bridge."

They exited to a small plaza. Directly ahead a tall tower with an archway flanked the end of a bridge. Instead of going through the archway, he led her through a tiny side door, then up a winding set of stairs inside the tower.

She emerged on top of the city. "Wow."

"This is Charles Bridge Tower."

Indeed. From every direction, she overlooked the red-tiled roofs of the city.

"Over there is St. Wenceslas Square, and the gold roof of the National Theater, where your show will be." He took her hand again, pulling her around to another side of the turret. "And on this side, a view of the Prague Castle and St. Vitus Cathedral."

The Gothic cathedral sat atop a hill, rising from inside a rectangular palace. Against the late afternoon sun, the black, ornate steeples and the giant curving cupola took her breath. "It's…"

"Even more amazing inside," he finished.

"Thank you for this."

"Oh, we're far from done."

He began pointing out the statues, relating the story behind each. He seemed delighted to share with her the mysteries of the city.

The wind rustled his curly hair, and she had to keep herself from running her fingers through it.

What—?

Okay, he was her bodyguard. She needed to remember that tidbit of information.

"…it's the best place to buy a souvenir, if you want. Or we can go right up to the castle."

She nodded.

"Which—get a souvenir or go see the castle?"

"Both."

They stopped on the Charles Bridge and watched the ferries, then hopped a trolley car for the ride up the hill. She lost herself in the crowd of onlookers, standing locked inside time as she pondered the cathedral.

"Imagine what it might be like to live with all this around you, all the time. All this beauty."

"I think people here start to take for granted what they have. It's easy to do when you're surrounded by it every day."

"I wouldn't."

He looked down at her, a strange look on his face. "No, I don't think you would."

They wandered through the palace courtyard. "I've always wanted to bring my family here to show them where I live."

"Why don't you?"

He stood, contemplating the steeples. "I have eight brothers and sisters. The airfare alone would break me. Then there's keeping track of them, although some are married and gone. Only Derek and Lucy are still at home."

"Lucy was the one at the concert in D.C.?"

He nodded. "She's a Vonya wannabe."

She made a face. "Sorry about that. I forget sometimes that I have influence over teenagers."

"You shouldn't. It's important. I just wish they could see what I saw today."

She looked away. She watched a family, the mother and father swinging their son between them. Her throat burned. She slipped her hand out from his. Enough of this silliness.

"Hey," he said. "You okay?"

She nodded. "Let's go."

He frowned. "What is it?"

She shook her head, hating the tears that brushed her eyes. If only—

"Are you crying?"

"Me? No. The sun's too bright."

"Give it up, Ronie. What's the matter?"

"It's just— Forget it."

He closed his mouth, a muscle pulling in his jaw. Then he reached again for her hand. "C'mon."

She let her grip go limp in his, but apparently he didn't care as he walked them through the courtyard and back to the bridge.

Her hand was sweating by the time he stopped her at a statue of St. Wenceslas, the sun bleeding pink and red into the horizon. A chill whipped up, beading her skin. "You know what you and he have in common?"

"We're both made of tin?"

"Funny. No. Wenceslas was known for his kindness to the poor. He could have wallowed in his pain—after all, his father died when he was thirteen, and he grew up with a mother who took the throne and tried to kill him. He had to overthrow his mother when he came to power, at the age of eighteen. But when he finally did, he defended the church, and Christianity spread. The Christmas song written about him was just a fairy tale, but what isn't a fairy tale is the fact that he was a good man."

"I still don't see the connection. No one has tried to kill me."

Oops. Wrong choice of words. But he shook his head. "That's the thing, Ronie. *You* have tried to get rid of who you are. You're so much like Wenceslas—doing good for others, helping the poor. But you do everything under a mask, hiding the *real* Ronie. Like you want her to disappear. What if you...what if you left it all behind and just performed as Ronie?"

She stared at him. "Because no one would listen. Can you even imagine that? Mousy me, behind a microphone? I'd be like that poor street musician over there." She pointed to a man with an accordion. "Could you give him a couple bucks? I'll pay you back."

Brody considered her a moment, then dug into his pocket and gave him two coins.

By the time he'd returned, she'd conjured up a response. "I'm not the only one hiding. What about you? And the fact that you can't stand Lyle? What's that about?"

"I like Lyle." His tone came out stiff.

"No, you don't. He annoys you. I noticed it that first morning you made breakfast. He raises all the hairs on the back of your neck and you can just barely be civil, right?"

"I think this tour is over." He reached for her elbow but she yanked it away.

"Nothing doing. You promised me food."

"I'll order you something at the hotel."

She pursed her lips. "Not on your life. I want to know what's going on."

"It's my job to understand you, not the other way around."

Oh. So that was what this was. An interrogation. She curled her arms around her body. "You're right. Maybe this wasn't a good idea. Take me back to the hotel."

That took the wind out of his sails. "Listen, I'm sorry. Lyle reminds me of someone…someone I hurt."

She saw it then, pain flashing through his eyes. She held out her hand. "I'm a pretty good listener, if you want to air out your thoughts."

A slow, measured smile crossed his face. "Fine. I'll tell you about it, on one condition."

"Is that a challenge?"

"Are you up to it?"

Will you catch me? The thought brought a flush to her

face. Oh, brother. See, that was what wandering around the city of romance did to a gal. Tangled her brain with unattainable ideas. Still, she nodded.

"Good. Come with me."

He had a plan, and it would only hurt a little bit.

The sun had begun to sink as he led her back to the square. He'd seen the way she'd eyed that seafood platter and, frankly, she needed something besides peanut butter.

Indeed, her eyes lit up just a little as they emerged onto the square and headed toward the restaurant. He found a table under an umbrella and pulled out her chair.

She smiled up at him, and again he felt that warm swirl inside. It was a lot nicer than the panic he'd felt when she'd said their tour of Prague had been a bad idea.

"You know what I want," she said to him when the waiter appeared, and he ordered her a big plate of seafood.

"I'll have pig's knuckle," he said, winking at her.

Winking? Oh, good grief. He needed to get himself under control. Ever since he'd gone rogue and offered to show her the city, he'd experienced a sort of out-of-body view of himself wooing her.

He was just trying to get her to loosen up. Be herself.

Not Vonya, not Veronica. Herself. A person he had a feeling he might know even better than she did.

"The clock is going to chime." Ronie pointed to the crowd gathering, and they watched as the clock rang the dinner hour and then the apostles rotated through the doors, ending with the golden rooster crowing.

She was smiling. Her smile, when it was authentic, could stop the world. And he longed for her to take off that cap and let him see her dark hair. Thankfully, she'd taken off her sunglasses, and the glow of the sunset lit up her incredible hazel eyes.

For Pete's sake, this town had gone right to his head.

"Okay, you got me here. Now, what's going on with you and Lyle?"

He'd hoped she'd forgotten that part. "He's a nice kid."

"Yes? And?"

"And he constantly wants me to play with him. Why is that, anyway?"

She shook her head. "It's about spending time with you. He doesn't have a father, and it doesn't take a genius to see he likes you. You're Superman to him. It's not going to hurt you to let him in your life."

But, oh, it could. He froze, closing his eyes against the voice from the past. *Hey, mister, kick me that ball!*

"Come back to me, Brody." Her touch jerked him out of the memory and he took a breath.

"What's going on?" she asked softly.

He blew out the breath and laid his hands on the table. "I… It's just a long story."

She leaned back and smiled.

It seemed that he just might do anything for Ronie's smile.

"I met him in Darfur. We were there for four months, helping with a refugee camp, protecting the health-care workers and distributing aid. It was a mess—no organization, families coming and going…" And aid workers. Shelby flashed into his mind and he blinked her away.

"There were kids everywhere—most of them orphans, a few with families. We didn't know who belonged to whom, or where they lived. Sometimes they'd hike for days to get food for their families—we'd see them hanging around, and then they'd take off again for weeks."

She leaned forward, settling her chin on her hand.

"It seemed they were always kicking around a soccer ball. Sometimes the guys and I would play with them, you know, just to pass the time." He watched the crowd behind her, glad, suddenly, for her in-plain-sight disguise. Otherwise he'd never let her sit out in public like this, unprotected.

"Simone was one of the kids who came in and out of our lives. We'd be playing soccer, then the next week he'd be gone. Then in a few days, back again. That last time, I didn't notice how long he'd been gone. It was chaos anyway—things were getting dangerous and the UN decided to pull out the aid workers. We were packing up to leave and Shelby just had to check on—"

"Shelby?"

He looked at her, at those sweet eyes, and swallowed.

And she knew. He saw it in the way her expression changed. A sort of sadness filled her face—which was strange because she certainly didn't care about his former—or, for all she knew, current—girlfriend. Right?

He drew in a breath. "An aid worker I knew. She wanted to help a patient, Mani, who had gone missing from the camp. Apparently, the woman lived in a village close by. So I let her convince me to borrow a Jeep and we took off. When we got there, soldiers were in the middle of a raid, setting homes on fire, killing women, stealing the boys. We got to Mani's tent and discovered her there with her two children, still alive. Shelby and I tried to get them to the Jeep but we were chased by a bunch of…of…" He wiped his mouth, staring up into the twilight.

"A bunch of…?" Ronie slipped her hand over his. He squeezed it, thankful for the increasing darkness.

"Soldiers. No—kids. Armed with AK-47s. The kind that get recruited into the army."

She stiffened.

Well, it was the kind of visual that might horrify anyone. And it got worse. "They surrounded our truck, shot Mani and then Shelby. Then a boy pointed a gun at one of the kids, and I just—I couldn't let that happen."

"So you shot him."

He nodded, wincing, turning away from one memory right into the next. "And then suddenly, there was Simone. He had a gun, too, and had come up beside me. He pointed it at my head."

Her mouth opened, and she closed it fast, her eyes big.

"I had those two kids, and Shelby was bleeding out. I knew if I didn't get away—"

"No one would live."

He nodded and let go of her hand. "So I grabbed his gun and threw it away. And then told Simone to run."

"But he didn't."

"I think he wanted to. I saw the fear, even the hope, in his eyes. And then I heard men shouting and knew we'd run out of time. I picked up the two kids and threw them in the car. I grabbed Shelby—her blood was everywhere. By that time, Simone had picked up his gun and turned it back on me. He pulled the trigger."

"And you shot him."

Why had he thought he could just spill out this information, that it wouldn't turn him inside out and destroy their evening? No—he'd never really intended to deliver the sordid truth until she'd mesmerized him with that smile, those eyes. And here he was, about to become a blubbering idiot in front of her. "I didn't know what else to do." He shook his head. "Shelby died on the side of the road, while I tried to field-dress her wounds."

She reached for his hand again and, heaven help him, he let her take it.

She squeezed and held on.

NINE

Ronie wanted to cry for him, but that wouldn't do either of them any good. She saw it all—saw him staring at this boy he'd come to care about, raising his gun and pulling the trigger.

She wanted to scream for him. Instead she held his hands in the fading twilight, wanting with everything inside her to put her arms around him and make it better. As if.

"Brody, I'm so sorry."

He wouldn't look at her.

"It doesn't help if I say you didn't have a choice, right?"

He shook his head.

She sighed. "I forgive you for not loving Lyle like I do. But if you ever wanted to give him a chance, you might be surprised."

He glanced at her then, a look in his eyes that made her want to cry.

She leaned back to let the waiter deliver her a heaping pile of shrimp, scallops and noodles, but she'd lost her appetite. She picked at her food, watching Brody pick at his.

Wow, did she want to make this better for him. "Thank you for telling me your story, Brody. I...I really do understand the feeling of being helpless, caught—wishing you could change the past."

He looked up at her then. "I know you do."

A band had begun playing inside the restaurant, the smooth sounds of jazz spilling out into the languid night. Overhead, the orange lights of the Gothic cupola looked down on her like the eyes of a jack-o'-lantern. Around the square, lights from the other restaurants sparkled.

Brody pushed his plate away. "Want to get out of here?"

"Not really, but—"

"You have to keep your part of the bargain, remember?" He raised an eyebrow and the look of mischief in his eyes had her pushing away her own food. Oh, this man could be dangerous to the spy girl inside.

Speaking of which...how could she betray him tomorrow night after everything he'd just shared with her? Maybe he didn't have to know she'd ditched him.

He took her hand in his. She'd started to think maybe it belonged there.

They disappeared into the winding, cobbled streets of Old Town. Strangely, no fear crept up her spine as they wandered in and out of dark shadows. She held on, drawing close, letting herself breathe in his husky, masculine smell.

What on earth was she thinking? At best they'd end this trip civilly. Most likely, after tomorrow night, he wouldn't speak to her again.

Maybe he'd even quit.

She took a shuddering breath.

"You okay?" He looked back at her. He had eyes that could turn a girl weak. Somehow she managed a nod.

"Good. Because I want to see the girl who threw a roll at me the first day I met her."

"Second, actually."

He grinned. "Actually, I think I'm just meeting her now."

Oh. Wow.

He pulled her into a café with tinny electric music and a few people on the dance floor. He led her toward the back, toward stairs that wound under the café.

"What's this?"

"Frankie's Underground. It's a blues club."

Her mouth opened in surprise. "Thought you'd approve," he said.

More of a cave than an underground room, the bar seemed chipped right out of the earth, with six or seven barrel tables and a couple of musicians shoved into a corner.

"I love it." She slid onto a stool.

He motioned to a waiter. "A couple of tonic waters."

The waiter nodded.

"You come here a lot?"

"When I'm in town. This guy here can play Coltrane like nobody's business. But they also do a good Otis Rush. And they're always happy to let others take the mike." He grinned at her again.

"Uh...wait. You don't think... Brody."

He patted her on the shoulder and went up to the guitarist.

She turned, shaking her head, but he was already

gesturing to her—no, pointing. Like she might be some wannabe blues singer—

He returned. "Do you know 'Downhearted Blues'?"

"You didn't."

He held open his arm, gesturing to the stage. "Don't get shy on me now, Vonya."

She shook her head but a swirl of delight made her slide off her stool. She looked up at Brody. "You want Vonya?"

Something flickered in his eyes. "I want to hear the real Ronie Wagner."

The real Ronie Wagner.

She walked up to the mike and grabbed it with both hands, looking over at the guitarist who'd moved to the keyboard. He wore an Irish cap and a black vest over a tight black T-shirt, and looked younger than her.

She nodded, took a breath, looked out at Brody and let the words curl out.

"Gee, but it's hard to love someone when that someone don't love you…"

Her voice sounded tinny and weak. She took a breath and dug deeper.

"I'm so disgusted, heartbroken, too. I've got those downhearted blues…"

Yes. She smiled at Brody as he leaned forward in his seat, perching his chin on his open palm. She lost herself in the slow, sultry rhythm, using her voice like an instrument, her tones sliding through the room.

"Once I was crazy 'bout a man—he mistreated me all the time…

"The next man I get has got to promise me to be mine, all mine!"

Brody sat up, actually looking uncomfortable. She threw her head back.

"Trouble, trouble, I've had it all my days. It seems like trouble going to follow me to my grave."

When she finished, she turned to the keyboardist. "Do you know 'It Had to Be You?'"

He nodded, and she began to sing her own version of the standard, improving a few lines just for Brody.

"Why do I have to do…just as you say?"

She winked at him. He shook his head.

"You always have to have your own way."

He crossed his arms.

"What is the game we have to play…"

As she sang Brody got up from the table. Oh—he wasn't leaving, was he?

"Why did it have to be you, to make me sing the blues…"

No, he was walking toward the stage. She grabbed the mike from the stand. "I wandered around until I finally found the man who could make me be…"

"True," he said with a smile, his hand closing over hers.

"And sing the blues!"

Brody wrestled the mike from her. "I think we've had enough from—"

"Some other big guys just might try to send me goodbye—"

"No wonder Tommy won't let you sing your own songs."

"Hey, I'm a great lyricist. Usually."

The music played on. He looked at the keyboardist, who nodded at him, and he put the mike to his mouth.

"But nobody else could give me a thrill…'cause… um…"

"You love me…still."

He shot her a look. "Are those the words?"

She shook her head, still warm from the feel of his baritone coursing through her. She'd left the real lyrics behind a long time ago. But it was all just for fun. Right?

"I love you…" he sang, his smile gone. He turned and put the mike back on the stand as the musicians finished the song. "Thanks, guys," he said, and reached out for her hand.

Then, without a word, he pulled her through the cavern, up the stairs and out into the street.

"Brody."

"Don't talk."

He led her down the darkened street, his hand tight in hers. "Brody, what's the matter?"

He stopped then, rounding on her as if he had something to say. But whatever it was, the words didn't make it past his mouth.

Because then, just like that, he kissed her, hard and fast, practically inhaling her as she leaned back against the stone wall of some ancient building.

Brody?

He had the most amazing smell, and a late-afternoon stubble that made her bring her fingers to his face.

She couldn't remember the last time she'd kissed a man, and even so, she'd never been kissed like this, like the world had dropped away around them.

Her hands found the collar of his shirt and she held

on, tasting the seltzer on his lips. He was so very strong as he grasped her upper arms and—

Pushed her away?

"Oh…" He held up his hand as if stopping something. "Oh, no. Oh, Ronie." He turned away from her, rubbing the back of his neck and stepping out into the street.

She flattened her hands against the wall, still trying to sort out what had happened, and why she hadn't had the urge to slap him—being in his arms twice before had elicited exactly that response.

But for a second there, she'd felt…normal. Even whole. Like this amazing, uncomplicated, kind man wanted her. The real Ronie Wagner. Not the pop star or political heiress but the girl who made up crazy lyrics and sang the blues.

"Brody—" Her voice shook.

"I'd better get you back to the hotel. You have rehearsal in the morning and your big show tomorrow night."

Her big show. Yes. "Listen—"

"No." He turned. Was he actually shaking? "No. I'm sorry. I don't know what I was thinking. I just…I wasn't, I guess. Whoa." He held up his hands in surrender and even backed away from her as if she might have a contagious disease.

And that felt great. She looked away before she started to cry.

"I'm sorry, Vonya. I should have never taken you out today. This went way too far."

Vonya. She nodded, praying the wind might dry her eyes. Yes—way, way too far.

"Can you forgive me?"

Yes. Because now, at least, she didn't have to spare a moment for guilt. Vonya could betray him and not even look back once.

Oh, he'd hurt her but good.

Brody stood in the stage wings, watching her on the stupid swing, and couldn't get the feel of her in his arms out of his mind.

Soft and sweet and willing to kiss him. And she'd even tasted sweet, the tonic water on her lips. She was small—he'd never realized, really, how small. Breakable, even.

And when she'd kissed him back, the world had stopped whirring and come to a complete, delicious, full stop. He could have stayed there in her arms forever.

"Brody, look alive. She's going back for her next costume change."

"Right."

Luke knew. He had to know, from the way Brody had come into the room, sat on the bed and cradled his head in his hands.

"Please don't tell me…" Luke had said finally, flicking on the light.

"Turn that off. Go back to sleep. Don't ask me anything."

Luke turned off the light. "I don't know why you're beating yourself up. You two are perfect for each other. You're both convinced you don't have time to fall in love. And you, pal, believe you don't deserve it. Which, by the way, you're wrong about."

Brody scooped up a pillow and threw it. Luke added it to his pile.

But really, he did think that—anyone who let a woman he cared about talk him into a blunder that cost her her life… No, maybe it wasn't about deserving. It was about not being that stupid ever again.

Your love gives me wings…

He walked around the back of the stage to the stairs underneath. After the song, she'd drop through a hole, then dash to the dressing area. He liked to be there, just in case.

Who was he kidding? He just liked being around her. Even as Vonya. Her creativity, her energy, her laughter— it all made him feel alive in a way he hadn't felt since long before Shelby. Okay, maybe never.

The music stopped, the applause thundered through the musical palace and Vonya appeared, running down the stairs. She hustled past without looking at him and slipped behind the dressing curtain. Leah helped her into her final costume, one of his favorite outfits—a black flapper dress with a white wig, feather boa and headband. It went with her "Cha Cha, Love You" song. At least that was what he called it since those were the only words he understood.

Still, it was his favorite, and the closest thing to capturing her true voice, in his opinion.

She shimmied past him, and he wished he could stop her and apologize. But the show had to go on.

She let the lift bring her onto the stage to more applause, and in a second she was belting out the last tune.

For a moment, he was back in the cavern, listening to those husky tones, feeling them winding through him.

He'd simply been taken with her voice—the way it

took over his thoughts, made him move to the stage. He'd never grabbed a microphone in his life.

This was what a woman did to a man. Made him think with his emotions.

He moved back to the wings to watch.

The worst part of all this had to be that he had absolutely nothing, nilch, *nichevo,* in common with Vonya. Shelby had been a healer, a rescuer. Vonya—he wouldn't call her Ronie again—was nothing but sheer chaos. Out of control.

Okay, there was Lyle. And the orphanage. And that Zimbalan tour that the media had made a fuss over. He'd spent the night looking her up on Google—and not because he couldn't get her out of his mind, thank you, but because he had to know just why she'd hang out with a guy like Damu.

He'd discovered plenty of pictures of her during the tour. A few had even made him smile, like the one of her trying to balance pineapples on her head. And, well, he supposed camouflage pants, a pair of high heels and a black netting top could be considered normal for Vonya. At least she had that body leotard under her outfit.

Which, he'd realized, she wore most of the time. Even in D.C., if he'd looked closely instead of assuming.

Okay, so he had made some very inaccurate assumptions about Vonya. From that first moment until now.

He remembered the woman he'd seen on Martha's Vineyard, and the woman her father had described. Did he even know his daughter?

Which led him to more Google searches, all the way back to her sister's death. Savannah had died of cancer at the age of twenty, and he'd found a number of pictures of her posted on an outdated MySpace page set up by Ronie.

Ronie had inherited her flamboyance from her sister, apparently, and had posted shots of her sister dressed in crazy getups—in fact, he'd seen a few of them on Ronie. And then there were shots of her singing, even at drama camp.

In fact, it seemed that Ronie had been every face of Savannah—but never just herself.

Why did it have to be you to make me sing the blues...

Until last night?

Her song ended and the stage faded to black. According to plan, she stayed in the shadows, and then, during the encore, let the lights come up slowly.

He waited for it watching as the spotlight slipped over her. She sparkled under it, a sizzling star.

He turned away as she sang her last song, a soft little melody that made her sound like Marilyn Monroe.

That Tommy D was a genius because, so help him, Brody had become a fan of Vonya—the crazy, kind, talented, fun performer.

But he didn't have to love her.

He'd keep his distance. No macchiato during rehearsal. No hunting down Nutella.

No late-night pizzas.

The last note faded out to thunderous applause. She waved and blew kisses to her audience, and finally the stage went dark. He expected her to walk off on his side, and when she didn't, he spoke into his mike. "I'm headed to her dressing room."

He'd just stand outside the door, of course. And then he'd walk her home.

And he probably shouldn't tell her that she knocked the audience out cold tonight.

Or that she looked amazing. And took his breath away.

Maybe, though, he'd mention how sorry he was for being a jerk.

And even promise never to kiss her again.

Or...not.

Yes! Definitely. He'd make that promise.

He went to her dressing room in the back of the palace. The light bled out from under the door. He could hear her inside, humming. Something soft. Bluesy.

"Downhearted Trouble." Or...no, something else.

He leaned against the door, trying to hear it but couldn't make it out.

It stopped.

Then started again.

That same humming, in perfect rhythm, without a change even in inflection.

"Ronie? Uh, Vonya?"

She kept humming.

He knocked on the door.

The humming stopped.

"Can I get you anything? A macchiato? A—"

The humming started again.

"Okay, listen, I'm really sorry for what happened. We probably need to talk about it. Tonight." He sighed. "How about if I track us down a pizza? I know a place on the other side of the river..."

More humming.

He grabbed the handle, knocking again. "I'm coming in there."

He turned it. Locked, of course. "Ronie, let me in."

Okay, that should have gotten some reaction. He put his shoulder against the flimsy door and banged. It shuddered.

Still she hummed.

"Ronie, if you're in there, you'd better clear the door." Then he stepped back and kicked right at the jamb, dislodging the ancient lock from the door. It banged open, hitting the wall behind it.

He followed it in.

The humming came from her iPod, set on repeat on the counter, under a row of hot lights.

But the room was empty.

"Luke, eyes on Vonya?"

"She exited the stage. She was heading toward the dressing rooms."

"She's not here." He ran down the hall and back up onstage. Tommy D was flirting with one of the stagehands. "Sorry to interrupt, TD, but have you seen Vonya?"

Tommy glanced at the redhead, winked. "I thought that was *your* problem, Boy Scout."

Oh, he wanted to hurt him. "Listen, she's gone, so if you know where she is—"

Tommy rounded on him, his smile gone. "She's not gone. She's here. Just calm down."

Brody shoved him away, turned, and nearly knocked over Leah. "Ronie's gone. Have you seen her? Do you know where she went? The truth, Leah."

He didn't need to waste his breath. Her wide eyes betrayed nothing but confusion.

He spoke into his mike. "Luke, I think our little songbird has flown the coop."

TEN

Of all the crazy moves Vonya had pulled, nothing compared to the insanity of standing in the dark corridor outside Tyn Cathedral, with only Brody's words for company.

How she wished he were standing here with her, if not holding her hand, at least close enough to hear her scream should someone jump out of the shadows.

Yeah, right. Like he would have come with her. After the way he'd shoved her away yesterday on the street, like he'd actually been repulsed...

She shivered, despite her leather jacket, jeans and boots. She'd pulled the feather headband from her hair and replaced it with a hat, although she'd kept the white wig.

And of course, she wore the red scarf around her neck, just as Bishop had said.

What a fool she'd turned out to be. To think a man like Brody might find her beautiful—she spent most of her time looking like other people. And that stunt in the blues café—that had been her playing, too, hadn't it?

No. For the first time, she'd let herself really sing. Let herself access what was deep in her heart. Why?

Because with Brody she felt safe. And real. And like she didn't have to put on an act.

She'd wanted him to kiss her.

Perhaps that had been the most foolish part of all.

What if you left it all behind and just performed as Ronie?

She'd let him egg her on. But he didn't understand. Being Ronie wasn't good enough. She had to be more. Or rather, she had to make up for what Ronie wasn't.

Out of all the people on earth, however, she'd thought he'd understand that.

She drew her coat closer around her. Perhaps she'd pinpointed the problem. *What kind of woman walks right into danger?*

His words from Damu's party can back to her, melded with his story about his lady doctor friend. Shelby? What if Ronie reminded him of the woman who had nearly gotten him killed? Who'd made him do the one thing that almost destroyed him?

See, she knew she couldn't tell him about tonight's adventure.

Little did Brody know that during their excursion yesterday, she been mapping out her route back to the square.

She pulled off her wig, shoving it into her pocket. She placed the cap over her curls.

Her hand curled around the computer in her pocket.

Where was Bishop's computer guru?

The cathedral door recessed back from the street in a sort of alleyway. It suddenly seemed too conspicuous a place to meet someone—in this closed space, where she might be trapped. And for her contact, too. Maybe he meant to meet her in the street.

She edged out and tucked herself in a pocket of shadow next to a restaurant.

The wind skittered leaves across the cobblestones, and she smelled rain in the air. A couple out late—a tall woman leaning heavily on her date—shuffled by. Across the square, Lyle's window light in the hotel flickered on. She looked for Brody's light, but his bedroom remained dark. She had no doubt Brody had ramped up the search to full rampage by now.

"Do you have a song for me?"

She startled at a young man who looked about eighteen, if that. A thin stocking cap half covered long, unruly dark hair, and he smacked his gum, probably to the beat pulsing through his earbuds. He held a backpack and looked the part of a student with a dark suit coat, collar up, over a T-shirt, and a pair of dirty tennis shoes.

"Did Bishop send you?"

"Whatya have?"

She looked for the red scarf and found the bandanna on his backpack. Relief shot through her. She dug into her pocket and pulled out the computer. "You're late—"

A crack shocked the air, and she jumped back as blood splattered her face, her neck, her hands.

The kid's head jerked back. He collapsed. His body spasmed on the sidewalk.

She stood there, unable to move. Or breathe. She needed...

Her hands shook as she stepped back and fell over a chair behind her, sprawling on the sidewalk.

The boy had stopped shaking, now lying with his eyes wide in the dim glow of a jewelry store's night display.

A second shot shattered the glass window beside her.

She screamed, diving out of the way, and crawled across the cobblestones as the glass spilled onto the sidewalk. She turned over, gasping, then hit her feet.

Her legs moved then, fast. She didn't know where she was running to—not toward the hotel, but away, just away, down the street.

She heard her own sobs ripping out of her, but she couldn't think and just kept moving. She ducked down another road, her feet loud against the cobblestones, turned into another alley and sprinted.

She emerged right out into the square, half a block down. She'd run in a circle—now what? She stood under the lamplight and held out her hands.

Blood, drying into the lines of her hands, splattered along her arms, her coat.

Sirens.

She backed up, pressing herself against a building, shaking.

An arm snaked around her, clamping over her mouth, hard, unforgiving. "I found you."

She felt a scream tear through her and went berserk, slamming a fist back into her captor's leg, landing her foot into his instep. He woofed out a breath, let her go, and she whirled, fully intending on jamming her fingers into the well of his neck.

He caught her wrist. "Ronie!"

She gulped a breath. Brody. Oh… "Brody!"

She launched herself, full on, into his arms, holding on with everything inside her.

And then, once again, he lifted her and carried her away.

"Where are you hurt?" He wanted to put her down, but if he wasn't mistaken, someone had just been shooting at her.

Shooting. He knew it. Why hadn't he listened to his instincts?

Oh, wait. He knew why. Because he'd become an idiot.

Brody tightened his grip around her—so tight he might never let her go—and lost himself in the winding streets of old-town Prague.

"Where are you hurt?" He didn't mean the anger in his voice—okay, he did, but not like that. It was more relief than anything. He'd get back to anger later.

Once he figured out if she was going to live. *Please, God.*

And yes, he'd actually prayed as he'd run out of the theater, after Artyom had caught her leaving the building on video. He'd taken a wild guess that she would head to the square—something about the way she'd been taking everything in on their tour had bothered him somewhere in the back of his brain.

Never did he expect to show up and see her across the square seconds before—she didn't actually shoot that kid, did she? Or…

He found a set of stairs leading into a building and

put her down on them. She shook, her face white. "Don't go into shock. Stay with me, honey."

But she had begun to crumple, her beautiful face tightening before she hid it in her—

"Your hands are bloody."

She looked up at him and he saw that her face bore traces of blood, too. "Please tell me you're not hurt."

"It's not my blood." Her voice emerged, whisper thin. "I…I didn't know him. Is he… I think he's…"

"He's dead." Indeed, Brody had reached him seconds after she bolted, and had stopped only long enough to check for vitals.

He'd called Luke as he sprinted after Ronie. Thankfully Luke hadn't asked any questions. Well, not yet.

"Ronie. Tell me what happened. What were you doing there?"

She shook her head, her gaze glued to her hands.

"Ronie."

"No!"

Okay, this wouldn't work. He needed to check her out, confirm for his panicked brain that, really, she wasn't bleeding and just couldn't feel it. But not here, not in this alley.

Not with the police on her tail.

He scooped her up again, and she curled into him, trusting him. About time. Then he stalked through the streets toward his apartment.

The lights of the Charles Bridge glared on the water, the city bright and dangerous as the sirens whined in the air. He stayed in the shadows, smiling at a couple tucked in a love knot as they followed him with their eyes.

He took the stairs off the side of the bridge and made his way to his tiny flat on Nosticova.

He punched in his code, took the stairs and dug the key out of his pocket.

The two-bedroom flat smelled like Luke's socks, but thankfully his roommate had left it clean. The night poured in through the double window in the main room. He kicked the door shut, then set her down on the leather sofa, closing the curtains.

Towels. He locked and bolted the front door on the way to the bathroom.

She sat hunched over, still trembling when he returned. He knelt before her, cupped her chin in his hand and wiped her face with the wet washcloth.

"Let me see your hands."

She held them out. Only a mild scrape remained after he washed off the blood. He'd seen that sheet of glass come down and thought...

He sucked in a hard breath. "Anything hurt?"

She kept her big eyes on him. "No." Actually, no noise came from her mouth—he had to read her lips, but he got it.

And then, because as long as they were out of their element, he sat on the sofa and carefully moved her into his lap. He curled his arms around her, and held her.

He sat there, probably too long, considering all the possibilities, expecting his anger to return, and was shocked when it didn't.

But he was okay with that, for now.

She drew her legs up in a ball, as if she might be trying to crawl inside his chest.

"Shh. It's going to be okay."

"That guy died."

Yes, finally, a voice.

"You didn't… I mean—" He cleared his throat. "I'm just going to ask once. You didn't have anything to do with his death, right?"

She pushed away from him, her eyes on his. "Yes. Yes, I did." She started to shake again.

Yes? "Shh. Okay, Ronie, calm down." He held her face in his hands, hating the coldness her words had stripped through him. "What do you mean?"

"It was my fault that he was there. My fault…and…" Tears now spilled down her face, her nose ran. "Who would want to kill him?"

"Uh…I don't want to suggest this, but what if the killer was after you? I mean, there was another shot."

"You know that? You were there?"

"Of course I was there." He left out the part about rabid fear. "That's my job. And if you had let me in on what you were doing—"

"I couldn't!" She bounced out of his lap, backing away from him. "See, that's the thing. I couldn't tell you because you would have stopped me."

"From doing what?"

She pressed her hands over her ears.

"I'm sorry. I didn't mean to shout. But tell me—what's going on here?"

She closed her eyes.

"Ronie, who was that guy?"

She turned her back to him.

Oh, brother. He crossed in front of her. "What were you doing with him?"

"He's with the CIA, okay?" She brought her arms

down, opening her eyes. "He's with the CIA. And…so am I."

He had nothing. He just stared, trying to actually comprehend her words. "You're…with the CIA? Like a spy?"

She made a face, lifted a shoulder. "Kind of."

"How can you be *kind of* with the CIA?"

"I sometimes courier information back and forth. The kind that they can't put in the mail. Or on the internet. It's a favor for—"

"A *favor?*" Now she should put her hands over her ears, because he fully intended to get loud. "A *favor.* For the *CIA?*"

"Could you not yell?"

"Get used to it, baby. And you might as well get comfortable, too, because I want you to start at the beginning—birth if you have to—and tell me the entire truth. If I even smell a whiff of a lie—"

"I won't lie to you anymore, Brody."

Her voice, so full of pain, stopped him cold. She backed up, and dropped on the sofa, folding her hands on her knees, giving him a pitiful expression.

His anger deflated right out of him.

Which left only fear.

Who was this woman?

Scared. Alone. And needing a friend from the looks of her. Finally, the real Ronie.

He wasn't sure, but he may have preferred the one in the club. At least then he'd been the one afraid. And he much preferred to manage his own fear than see her so deeply shaken.

He took a kitchen chair, turned it around and strad-dled it. "I'm listening," he said softly.

She took a deep breath, licked her lips and didn't meet his eyes.

Outside, the sirens had died. In his pocket, his cell phone vibrated. *Not yet, guys.*

"Can I have a drink of water?"

He got up, grabbed a bottle from the fridge and handed it to her.

She spilled it down her chin, wiping it with her hand. "It all started in Zimbala."

No, it had started with her sister's death, but he didn't correct her.

"It was a goodwill tour, through Care for the World Ambassador, to raise awareness of the refugee camps and bring in aid.

"I'd already been sponsoring a child in Zimbala through CWA, so I thought I'd try to meet him. He wasn't at the refugee camp, so I bribed our guide to help me find him. We finally tracked him down at a work camp, where General Mubar offered 'jobs' to the locals. They were building some sort of camp. I found out later that he was making one of their many diamond mines. Of course, he didn't know I'd gone—"

"You were in disguise."

"Yes. I couldn't believe Kafara was working there—I thought he was in a school. At least that was what I was paying for. He told me that General Mubar had taken all the boys over nine years old out of the school to work. I knew I had to get him out of there, so I went to the embassy. They did absolutely nothing about it, but later that week, a man named Clive Bishop contacted me."

"He said he was with the CIA."

"Yes."

"And you believed him?"

"He seemed legit. And trustworthy. He wanted to help and I had no reason to suspect he was lying. He told me that if I helped them by carrying information, he'd help me by getting Kafara out of the camp and eventually to America, where I could adopt him."

"So you agreed."

"It was a digital file. They'd packaged it into a pair of earrings and I wore them home. Easy."

He saw, for a second, the same girl who had picked up a roll and pitched it at his head, the same one who had grabbed the mike last night, a moment before *Why did it have to be you? To make me sing the blues...*

Head in the game, Brody.

"And?"

"I thought, mission accomplished. Only, by the time Bishop went to the camp, Kafara had disappeared. He's spent the past two years trying to locate him."

"While you've been acting as delivery girl."

"Hey, what did they say after 9/11? We need to return to real intelligence, the kind on the ground? And that everyone needs to be a part of protecting America?"

"You could have gotten killed."

"For a good cause."

He held up his hands in surrender before he said something he shouldn't.

She reached for the water again, keeping her big eyes on him as she took another sip. "Kafara was 'drafted' into Mubar's army."

Brody stiffened, refusing the images that wanted to enter his head.

"Bishop found him, and sent me a text when he found out about my trip. He has long suspected that Damu is smuggling diamonds out of the country, a side gig for the Mubar family fortune. The problem is, the diamonds are showing up in America and no one knows how. Damu and I really do happen to be friends—well, if you call our mutual distrust friendship. Or, maybe Damu really does trust Vonya, I don't know. He often tracks me down when I'm in Europe, and I've attended his birthday party the past two years."

"Does Leah know about your involvement with the CIA? Because she certainly didn't want to tell me you'd gone to his party."

She nodded.

"And Tommy?"

"No. He's like you. He doesn't like me hanging out with Damu. He'd—"

"Lay his body in front of a bus to stop you?" He said it straight out, angry and harsh.

She stared at him.

Okay, maybe that had been a little over the top.

"So, Bishop said he'd get Kafara out if you got close to Damu in hopes of finding the smuggler? How?"

When Brody found this Bishop fellow, he was going to get to him, teach him about what happens to people who used coercion techniques on civilians. Even willing ones.

"Damu and I often run into each other at parties. Bishop wanted me to use one of these opportunities to get Damu's cell phone, so he could get his contacts and sent messages. He sent me a V-chip copier, and I was supposed to lift his cell, copy it and slip it back into his pocket. Only…"

She reached inside her pocket and pulled out what looked like an iPhone. "It's one of those mini personal computers. I picked the wrong pocket."

"You took this off him?"

"While we were dancing."

Really, she had the capacity to astound him. He turned it on. A password prompt flickered onto the screen.

"The man I met tonight…Bishop sent him to hack the computer. I was just going to pass it off and be done with the whole thing."

She tried to put the cap on the bottle. It fell off and went spinning across the floor.

He sat back in the chair, staring at the computer. Keep her out of the tabloids, keep her out of trouble and bring her home in one piece. Maybe he'd get one out of three?

"So you see, now I need to find out who this smuggler is, or Kafara is going to die in Mubar's army."

The door banged open behind them.

Ronie jumped to her feet. Brody had already moved in front of her.

"It's just us, Wick." Luke stalked into the room followed by Artyom. And surprise, surprise, Vicktor Shubnikov, co-founder of Stryker International, came next in line, annoyance written on his dark Russian features.

And, behind him—oh, no.

"This is what you call R & R?"

Great. "Welcome home, Chet."

ELEVEN

"You mean to tell me she's been lying to you since you started this gig?"

Couldn't Chet just keep his voice down?

Brody had just given him all the details of the past few weeks, including Ronie's explanation of being involved in the CIA. Chet was clearly having a hard time grasping it all.

It sounded insane, even to Brody's ears. However, his tiny apartment wasn't exactly soundproof—he could practically hear Luke breathing on the other side of the bedroom wall. And thanks, he didn't want everyone on the Stryker team to know how Vonya had snowed him.

Brody drew a long breath before he made this conversation any louder. "Sort of. Yes."

"And you had no clue about any of this?"

Thank you, oh so much, boss, for pointing that out. As if he couldn't feel worse. "Except a gut feeling that she hadn't shown all her cards, uh, no. I mean, really— you've seen her act. Would you suspect her of working for the CIA?"

How he wanted to go on, to point out the obvious,

that Vonya built her persona on the unexpected—which, now that he thought about it, probably pegged her as the perfect CIA cover. And, despite all that, he *had* located her tonight…well, okay, maybe he wouldn't bring that up.

He couldn't nail down one good excuse for the way she'd outwitted him. Except, of course, for the obvious.

He'd let a woman screw up his brain, again.

Chet narrowed his eyes at him, as if trying to read Brody's mind. And not in a nice way, either. Tanned, wearing loose jeans, flip-flops and a Hawaiian shirt, his dark hair cut wedding short, a growth of beard—his boss had the appearance of a man annoyed because he'd had his honeymoon derailed.

Hey, who took month-long honeymoons anymore, anyway?

Thankfully, his new bride, Mae, had been kinder when she'd breezed in, delivering a change of clothes for Ronie, and when they didn't fit, calling Vicktor's wife, Gracie.

Gracie's jeans and black hoodie nearly swallowed the woman.

The three women now sat in a huddle on the sofa in the living room while Grace and Mae quizzed Vonya on her amazing life. Of course, both knew exactly who Vonya was. And, surprise, surprise, "Your Love Gives Me Wings" seemed to be a hit with the women on the team.

Chet cut his voice low. "Okay, let's sort this out."

Brody sat on the bed, suddenly achingly tired. So bone tired he could probably dissolve into a puddle in the middle of his double bed. Now that the adrenaline had worn off, he just wanted to throw his arm over his eyes and pretend he hadn't just nearly seen Ronie killed.

That he'd nearly had his heart ripped from his chest.

Again.

Chet took the desk chair, turned it around and sat on it. "Why did you take this gig in the first place?"

Why? Boredom, maybe. Cash, definitely. "I don't know. At first, I thought it would be easy money. Then I met her. Did you know she's the daughter of a senator? And her only sister died after Ronie gave her a kidney. Talk about a blow. But she's different than anyone you've ever met. She plays the role of this pop star, but really, she's quiet and kind and she has this amazing voice…"

And the softest dark brown hair, and when she laughed, it had this power to clear every thought from his head. Not to mention the way she smiled at him, and listened to him, turning over his words like they mattered, and—

"Wick?"

Oh. He'd stopped talking. Chet had his mouth pressed in a tight line. "Do you have feelings for this woman?"

"What? No. Of course not. But she needs our help, and I want to give it."

Chet ran his hands down his face. "Half of Prague is out there, searching for a woman who killed a kid in the middle of Old Town Square, and I come home to find out it's someone Stryker International is supposed to be protecting! What am I supposed to think here?"

"She didn't do it! Trust me, I was standing right there—"

"I don't want to even think about that. Wick, this is not your style. You're the guy who has all his *t*'s crossed, his *i*'s dotted. If there's anyone I can count on to get the job done without it getting personal, it's you. What's going on?"

So much for his team not hearing this.

Brody got up, turning to watch the dawn press away the night over the city. "I don't know. She just…" He took a breath, rounding on Chet. "Listen, you're one to talk. Who's the guy who snuck into a country in the middle of a civil war to rescue a woman he supposedly didn't love? Not to mention a country where he was a wanted man? Let me talk to *that* guy, because maybe he can help me figure this out."

Chet considered him for a long moment, during which Brody wondered if he should start working on a new résumé. Finally, a wry smile escaped. "Fair enough. You don't have to figure this out. But we do have to get a grip on what Stryker International is going to do next. Because the last thing we can afford is our names on the front page, connected with a murder investigation. You know we're already struggling."

Brody nodded. "I'm right there with you, boss." He went to the door, cracking it open. Luke and Artyom had gone back to the venue to take Leah and Tommy to the hotel after Brody's decree that everyone stay at the concert until his return.

Whoops.

Vicktor stood at the stove, his shirtsleeves rolled up, cooking something Russian with too much garlic—maybe fried potatoes and onions. His wife, Gracie, her blond hair long and pulled back into a ponytail, sat next to the open window. Mae had curled up with a pillow on one end of the sofa.

Ronie sat against the other end, her eyes on the door. She looked at him and he gave her the barest of smiles. *Hang in there.*

She drew her knees in and hugged them to her chest, looking frail and breakable in the wan morning light. He didn't like this side of her one wee bit.

He closed the door, turning back to Chet. "I think we need to get into this computer, see what it tells us. Can't hurt. At least we'll have the lay of the land and some leverage over this Bishop fellow." Whom he couldn't wait to get his hands on.

"I don't know, Wick. My gut says we should cancel this last concert, put Vonya—"

"Ronie. Her name is Ronie—"

"—on a plane and be glad we all got out of this alive, without our reputation being shot to bits."

"Which brings me to another glaring question. Who was doing the shooting tonight? Her father thinks General Mubar is after her, and frankly I'm not so sure he isn't right. Damu could have followed her to Prague, hunted her down—"

"You said Damu went to Paris."

"I think we need to check on that. I'm telling you, Chet, someone was shooting at her—someone was trying to *kill* her."

He looked up. Ronie stood at the door, her eyes wide. "Uh…I didn't mean to barge in. Your friend made us some food."

He grabbed the door before she could close it, pulling her inside. He put his hands on her shoulders, wishing he could pour into her everything he couldn't quite put into words. Like, the fact that if she'd been shot tonight—

Well, his voice probably did it for him. "Listen. Someone wanted to hurt you tonight, Ronie, and you *can't* ignore that. Chet thinks we need to pull the plug on the entire tour, and I'm not against that in the least."

She stared at him as if he'd slapped her. "What? No. I'm not giving up on this tour." She glared at Chet. "I don't know who you are, but you can just stay out of this."

Chet's eyebrows went up. "I'm Chet Stryker. Brody's boss."

"Oh. Well, Brody's boss, you should know that none of this is Brody's fault. I'm the one who sneaked away from him—twice—"

"Twice?"

"He didn't know about Damu's party," Brody said quietly. Perfect. Hopefully she'd keep quiet about the airport.

"Well, it's not like I'm easy to keep track of. I specialize in disguises—I mean, I even fooled him at the airport. He walked right past me."

Nice. "You can stop talking now, please."

She put her hand to Brody's chest, pushing him away. "But he found me tonight—I don't know how, maybe he's some sort of trained military tracker or something—"

No, he'd gotten lucky on that one, something that still filled him with a cold terror.

"And I probably would have died if he hadn't found me. I would have run right into that square and into the shooter's sights and…" She closed her mouth, her head still moving as if trying to find her next words, but Chet stood, holding up his hands in surrender.

"You don't have to convince me of Wick's ability to protect you—*if you work with him.* But we simply don't have enough information to even start figuring out who might want to hurt you, and continuing on tour is simply too dangerous, especially if you keep trying to sneak off behind his back."

"I'll start cooperating. I'll do *everything* Brody tells me to do. I won't go anywhere without him a foot away from me. I'll stay at home at night, knitting if he wants me to. But I am finishing my concert tour. And, thanks, but I'll take my computer back, too."

Brody couldn't stop the harsh chuckle. "Nice, Ronie. Like I couldn't see through that."

She actually looked hurt. "I'm serious."

He narrowed his eyes, gave her a shake of his head. "Really, you are good."

She sighed. "Okay, I guess I deserved that. But please, Brody, just give the computer back. I really will behave. But at the very least, I have to contact Bishop and have him set me up with another hacker. It's important to national security."

"It's important to *you*. And…that's enough for me."

It gave him some solace that he could surprise her, too.

"But we're *not* contacting Bishop. For all we know, he's in on this. After all, he knew where your contact would be. He could have sent the shooter," Chet said.

He saw the truth of it ripple across her face, even as

she shook her head. "No. Bishop has never steered me wrong."

Brody saw Chet's expression out of the corner of his eye.

But what if she was right? What if it wasn't Bishop?

Chet lifted his phone from his pocket. "We just happen to have our own hacker right here on staff with Stryker International." He met Brody's eyes as he spoke into the phone. "Privyet, Artyom. We need your mad skills."

He was going to help her?

Really?

Ronie sat on the sofa in a tight ball and watched as Brody argued with his team about how to protect her in Amsterdam while they figured out just who might be trying to kill her.

Kill. Her.

No. It had to be an accident. She stared at her clean hands, overly scrubbed, and clenched them tight, seeing that poor boy crumble in front of her. And worse, she might have blown her only chance to rescue Kafara. She pressed her hands to her mouth.

"Stop thinking about it." Brody, who'd apparently had one eye on her—would he not, from now on?—came over and sat on the coffee table. He took her hands from her face and held them between his. She'd forgotten how warm they were. "It'll get easier. Right now, you'll think about it every five seconds. But in a week or two, it'll go down to once or twice an hour. The key is to take control of your thoughts. Think of happy moments to replace the horrific ones."

Happy moments. Like the moment when he'd sung *I love you?* Even if it had been against his will?

She'd avoided that moment until now, but as he looked at her, compassion in his beautiful eyes, she let herself return to the club. Let herself hear the words come out of his mouth, almost like a question.

But he didn't love her. He'd loved another woman and lost her. He wouldn't make that mistake again.

"Is that what you did? You know, to forget…?"

He drew in a breath and looked at their hands. "I'll never forget."

No. Probably he wouldn't.

"Listen." He hooked a finger under her chin and tipped her face up to his. "Did you really mean you'd behave if we went to Amsterdam? Because I don't think I can take another night like tonight. Speaking of things I'll never forget, I'll always have imprinted in my head the visual of you diving to the pavement while glass rained down over you, believing in my heart I'd find you shredded and bleeding out." He stared at her hands, rubbing his thumbs over them. "Please don't do that to me again."

"I won't." Really? Oh, she hoped so, at least. But what about Kafara?

"You don't always have to save the world," he said, as if reading her thoughts. She opened her mouth to speak but he stopped her. "It's not your fault that your sister died, and it's not your responsibility to somehow make up for it, or try to take her place."

She frowned at him.

"I saw pictures of Savannah. I know she liked to dress up, play a part. I have a feeling Vonya is more Sav—"

"Ronie, do you have a listing of your concert dates over the past year?" Artyom looked up from where he sat at the kitchen bar, the minicomputer connected to his laptop with a cable. He'd broken into the computer with a few keystrokes. Of course.

Brody kept his eyes glued to hers, but she broke away. No, her crazy life didn't have anything to do with Savannah's lost dreams.

"Why?"

"I'm tracking Damu's email correspondence. There are a number in his trash file, all to the same person. I can't read the actual text, but a couple of weeks ago, when I was looking for possible threats to you, I was matching ticket recipients to venues and dates, and it seems that a number of these email dates correspond to your concerts. Do you know anyone called SAM613?"

"Seriously?" She looked at Brody. He met her gaze as if yes, she had the answer. "Of course not."

"And, hey, there are a couple here to that same address when you were at that CWA event in Paris last fall."

What didn't he know about?

Artyom turned around. She considered him the quiet one, with his knowing, dark eyes and a rare smile, his intellectual air. "Just think about this for a second. You've seen Damu a number of times this past year."

"Yes."

"And isn't it interesting that he happens to be in the same places you are?"

"He's a playboy. He travels. Has big parties. And a few times, he had his events scheduled long before I did. Like his birthday party. He didn't know I'd be in Berlin."

"Didn't he? Couldn't someone have sent him the information?"

"Who?"

"I don't know…Tommy?"

"Are you kidding me? Tommy doesn't even like Damu. He always tells me to stay away from him." She found her feet.

"That's true," Brody said. "Besides, you vetted him, right, Artyom?"

"Okay, how about Leah? She's your assistant, she knows your concert dates long in advance. She could send them to Damu—"

"Are you saying that Leah is a *diamond smuggler?*"

Artyom made a face. "I'll keep looking." He turned back to the computer. But Brody got up. "How about a member of the band? Or her road manager?"

"What if it's a coincidence?"

"There is no such thing as coincidence in the security world." Chet looked over at her from where he sat at the table, reading the security reports. "You were there. Damu was there. He was communicating with someone—the same someone—during every one of your dates. You took something off him, and a week later, someone takes a shot at you and kills your contact."

She flinched.

"Nothing is coincidental. You're in trouble, and if we hope to keep you alive, then we have to suspect everyone. We draw the line at no one. Not even your best friend."

The room went quiet.

She swallowed.

Artyom turned around again. "Her next stop is Amsterdam. Now that I have Damu's email, I can nose around, find his itinerary. I'll bet Damu is headed there. This doesn't have to be hard. We find Damu and stick to him until he passes off the diamonds to the smuggler. Make sure he doesn't get near Ronie." He glanced at Brody as he said it, and followed with, "And Brody will keep her alive."

He squeezed her hand.

Again, silence.

"Please." She met Brody's eyes. "*Please?* If we catch the smuggler, then Bishop can focus on rescuing Kafara, right?"

Chet got up, walked to the window and stared out into the pinking sky. "Okay, we'll go to Amsterdam."

Yes, yes!

Chet turned his dark eyes on her. "Ronie, you'll do your final concert. But there's no *we* here—Ronie, you will do *everything* Brody says, and he won't be more than a foot away from you for the rest of the tour. You'll get back to the States in one piece, and if we're lucky, we'll also figure out who might be smuggling diamonds into America." Okay, so there was something to the boss thing—he exuded an aura of don't-mess-with-me. "But this thing goes south at all, and you're on the first plane to the States. You're the number one priority, got it?"

She drew in a breath. No, Kafara was.

And when Brody met her eyes, he knew it, too.

TWELVE

Brody lay down on his bed like a normal person might, staring at his ceiling, listening to his heartbeat in his ears.

How was he supposed to trust her when she looked at him with that hollowed-out longing in her eyes? Her lips may have agreed to Chet's terms but Brody had no illusions that if she had to sacrifice herself to help Kafara…

Yes, this assignment had *pain* written all over it. And he had begun to realize that it wasn't just hers.

How he wanted to get his hands on Bishop, or just lock Ronie up in a hotel room and go after Kafara himself. And what guarantee did he have that Kafara even wanted saving? He'd seen those kids, the determination in their eyes—

They'd been brainwashed into a mind-set of violence. She might discover that Kafara had turned into a murderer.

A smart security agent, one who listened to his gut, would put her on the first plane home. But then again, he had never followed his gut well.

And it didn't help that she'd looked so pitifully hopeful

when he said that he'd help her get Kafara back. What was he supposed to do with that?

You have feelings for this girl, don't you?

Chet's voice burrowed into his thoughts. No. Of course not. So, she'd gotten inside a little…and yes, it had been a mistake to kiss her, and maybe they should talk about that…

He kept hoping that moment might just fade away… but being with her in Prague, seeing it through her eyes, had helped him see it also—the fairy tale of the castles, the hanging roses, the linden trees. He heard the music of the city, and the food—it even tasted better with her around.

It had to be you…

Stop. He needed sleep. And with Ronie tucked onto the sofa for a nap and the doors bolted, surely he could allow himself to nod off…

Except that every time he closed his eyes, he saw her standing in the shadows, heard her scream ripping through the midnight hour, followed by the shatter of the glass window onto the sidewalk. Then more screaming, filling the chambers of his chest, his heart—

Screaming.

"No! No! Stop!"

Brody sat straight up, opening his eyes. He *had* nodded off. And the screaming emanated not from his nightmares but the next room, where Ronie napped on the sofa.

Or was being torn limb from limb.

He hit the ground running, flew through the doorway and saw her thrashing with a blanket he'd given her after Chet and Mae and the rest of the Stryker team left, leaving behind Luke who'd crashed in the other bedroom.

She had the blanket wound around her arm, the other arm up around her head.

"No!"

"Ronie, wake up!" He sat on the sofa next to her, grabbing her shoulders. "Ronie!"

She opened her eyes, unseeing. He caught her arm as it nearly sideswiped him. "Ronie, it's just a dream!"

Her eyes focused then and she began to shake. "Oh, Brody. I'm sorry. Oh…"

What was he supposed to do? He pulled her to him, putting his arms around her. "Shh. It's over."

Still she trembled as she laced her arms around his waist. She seemed cold, shivering as she buried her face into his chest.

The sun filled the room with golden light. Yes, he'd most definitely nodded off.

He ran a hand down her hair, soft and smooth, breathing in her scent. Oops. Didn't mean to do that. She smelled of soap, with the faintest hint of her herbal shampoo. Like roses, maybe. "Is it that dream again, the one you had in Germany?"

She nodded and sank into him. Well, if she just wanted to let him hold her, he wouldn't argue. She was alone, after all, and just needed a friend.

"Do you want to talk about it?"

She said nothing as she shuddered. Finally, she pushed away. "The dream…it's so real. And horrible."

He touched her face, running his thumb down her sodden cheek. "Is it the same one you had before? The pineapple dream?"

One side of her mouth quirked up, as if she found a sort of humor in his question. "Yes. The pineapple dream. Although it's not really about pineapples. See, when I visited Kafara, a woman would come every day, carrying this burlap bag on her head, filled with pineapples. I'd give him money and he'd buy me a pineapple. Then—he loved to show me this trick—he'd take her machete and cut it apart, right in his hand. I loved the fresh pineapples—I ate one every day." She looked up at him. Her smile fell. "In my dream, when Kafara slices the pineapple, it bleeds."

"Bleeds?"

"Yes. Like he's chopping up...I don't know, maybe something living. It's horrific. And I just know it's because he's being forced to..." She shook her head and hid her face in her hands.

He wrapped his arms around her again. She let herself be molded against him, and she fit like she'd always belonged there.

A spurt of fresh panic filled his chest. *Do you have feelings for this woman?*

He couldn't, could he? Feelings for Vonya?

No, not Vonya.

Ronie. The woman who cared so deeply about a little boy she'd only met briefly three years ago that she would risk her life for him. Be tortured with nightmares about him. She gave the best of herself to her career, her family.

Her friends.

Perhaps she deserved the best of him.

He rested his chin on her head and couldn't believe the words forming in his mind. "You have to swear to me that you'll keep your word to Chet, Ronie. We both know that if you want to, you can sneak away again, try to contact Bishop, or even track down this smuggler, and so help me, if you do that…"

"You'll send me back to America?" She lifted her head to look at him.

No, he'd lose his mind with worry. But he wouldn't tell her that. He pursed his lips and looked away. "Just, please—trust me." He hated how much pleading filtered through his voice.

Her palm on the center of his chest, warm and solid, made him look back at her. The morning sun caressed her face and for a moment, she appeared so…well, he had her in his arms already, didn't he?

He leaned close, everything inside him aching to kiss her. He heard the warnings in the back of his mind even as he cupped her face. But he didn't care. Not when she smiled so sweetly. "I do trust you," she said softly. "I won't make you watch me die."

He closed his eyes and leaned away. That was right. See, she could *die* if he didn't stay on his game, didn't do his job right, let her talk him into her crazy, secret, dangerous side trips.

Just like Shelby.

He knew that this thing had *hurt* written all over it. But he understood the nightmares, too. He had his own moments where he awoke, nearly screaming, in a cold sweat.

Perhaps, in fact, no one really understood her quite like he did.

She touched his face, her fingers soft and cool. "Please forgive me for betraying you."

He opened his eyes and found her gaze almost too much to bear. Somehow, he nodded. "I do. But you could have told me."

Her eyes narrowed and after a moment, she shook her head.

"Okay, maybe not. But I do understand. And I'll do whatever I can to make sure Kafara is freed."

She bit her lip, turned away. "Thank you."

"But promise me no more tricks. Every word I say, you hear me?"

"Yes, boss."

He couldn't shake the desire to kiss that nose. And that mouth. And what would that do for them? His job would end with her last gig—and she'd go back to America, while he'd stay in Prague.

Only he'd never again be able to enter his apartment without thinking of her in it.

"I know you're tired. And the flight doesn't leave for a few more hours. I think you should try to get more shut-eye."

She shook her head. "I'm afraid to sleep. It'll come back."

"What if I stay here?"

"You're going to protect me from my nightmares, too?"

"If I have to."

She sighed, straightening her blanket. "Brody Wickham, you're much too good at your job." Then she took his hand, wove her fingers into his and closed her eyes. "What am I going to do without you?"

What am I going to do without you? Ronie hated the words even as they came out of her mouth. What *was* she going to do without him?

She didn't have to think about that now, did she? Not when every time she closed her eyes she saw that poor boy's face as he crumpled to the ground. Or worse, when she did fall asleep, Kafara and his bloody machete.

Stop. Clearly, she'd come to rely—way too much—on Brody's hand in hers.

Probably a gal needed to remember that he was paid to hold her hand.

Paid.

Paid.

I love you…

No, he didn't. She'd practically forced him to sing those words, and so what if he'd turned to her not two minutes later and kissed her like he'd meant it, like she might be more than…

A client. Which apparently he'd come to his senses about shortly thereafter, because he'd pushed her away with a look of horror on his face.

She let his hand go. He withdrew it, of course. Because he was *paid* to hold it. Because she was his *client*.

She pulled the covers up to her shoulder and rolled over, listening to the beat of her heart—idiot, idiot, idiot. Vonya, even Veronica, was smarter than this.

And she'd promised to obey him. What was she thinking?

"Are you okay? Because you seem—"

"I'm fine." She closed her eyes and felt him start to move.

"Brody?" Wow, she'd turned into a glutton for punishment. But she didn't want him to leave. Not just yet. She rolled back to face him. "Why don't you work in America?"

He settled beside her, bracing his arm on the back of the sofa. He seemed to search her face for a moment. "Because there are a lot of people who need our help here. And America hardly feels like home anymore. Too many people living lives that feel out of touch with mine."

"Out of touch?"

"Families. Mortgages. Their lives feel so big. Complicated, even. This is enough for me."

This? His bare, simple two-bedroom flat, the stainless-steel kitchen, the leather sofa—a look at his life told her that Brody was exactly the guy he presented himself to be. Simple. Bold. Strong.

He didn't play games.

Which meant that whatever feelings he might have expressed for her—at the club, or even tonight when he'd woken her from the dream and held her...

No, Ronie. His job—he was just doing his job.

"This is enough?" She didn't meet his eyes, not sure why she'd even asked that.

"Sometimes."

Sometimes.

But that was it, wasn't it? Sometimes was all people like him could ask for. People who carried around wounds and kept scrambling just to keep up. People who were terrified to reach out for more.

You think you don't deserve to fall in love. Leah's voice reached out to her and took hold in her heart. Maybe. Yes.

Still, if Ronie did ever fall in love, she might consider a man who didn't play games. Who made her feel...safe. A man who made her believe that she didn't have to try so hard.

Yes, she wanted more than sometimes. She wanted a world of always.

THIRTEEN

"The Dutch have a saying, you know. God created the world but the Dutch created the Netherlands." Ronie slid open the drapes in her hotel window overlooking Dam Square.

"I think you might be Dutch. You have to be in charge of everything," Leah said.

"Funny." Brody sure knew how to pick hotels—this one had a view of the palace, with its neoclassical façade, and beyond that, the National Diamond Exchange.

She wasn't exactly deaf—she'd heard the conversations Brody and his team had quickly had during the trip to Amsterdam about tracking Damu, about him pawning off the diamonds in a place where they could be mixed with legitimate stock.

A place like the National Diamond Exchange.

If only Bishop would return her call. She'd like him to weigh in on Brody's plan—the one that included parking them two blocks away from the Exchange, in hopes of finding and following Damu, maybe tracking down his contact. Rescuing Kafara.

Oh, how she wanted to tag along with the Stryker team as they followed Damu. However, she knew Brody too well. He would lie in front of a bus before he'd let her near Damu.

And frankly, she couldn't bear to see him hurt. Not after what he'd gone through with Shelby.

"I love Holland. Have I ever mentioned that?" She turned to open her suitcase.

"A few times." Leah set a folder on the desk, next to the faux animal-print chair. Gold wallpaper and a dark walnut headboard made Ronie feel as if she were in a box of dark Dutch chocolates.

"Oh, I love the windmills," Leah said in her best Ronie imitation. "And can I get a bicycle?" She batted her eyes at Ronie.

"Funny. But I do want a bicycle. Imagine being able to cycle everywhere, over the cute little bridges, in front of the canals, with the houses tucked side by side like a Christmas village."

"You can only bicycle because there are no hills in Holland. It's a pancake. You'd get to a hill and call for a taxi. By the way, I put in an order of *Stroppewaffles* at the front desk. You know they're pure sugar, right?" Leah asked.

"Stop. Keep me in my dream world where caramel and waffle sandwiches are good for you."

"Fine, live large. You'll be dieting when you can't fit into your costumes anymore."

"I've been thinking about that. What if Vonya's next album is all blues covers. Like 'God Bless the Child' or 'I'll Be Seeing You.'" She hummed a few bars. "Maybe we'll nix the funky outfits."

"I think your fans would think you've lost your mind."

"I could wear dresses from the twenties, like my flapper dress. I love that costume."

"You're not the only one."

Ronie glanced at her. "What are you talking about?"

Leah smiled. "Nothing. I think Lyle would like to go to that carnival tonight, maybe after the concert?"

Ronie glanced outside again, at the bedazzled Ferris wheel in front of the palace. "I'll have to ask Brody. But probably that will work."

"You and he have barely left each other's side since Prague. I mean, he's a little obsessive, isn't he? He even stood outside the bathroom in the airplane today."

This was why she should have told Leah about the shooting. But Brody and the Stryker team had her on lockdown. She couldn't breathe a word, in case she had some terrorists in her company. Who did they think wanted to kill her—Lyle?

"Brody's just doing his job."

"I think he's more than doing his job. I wouldn't be surprised if he had a glass to the door right now." She leaned toward her bedroom door, which led to the bigger suite. "Hear that, Mr. Bodyguard? You're creeping me out."

Ronie laughed. The whole thing seemed so unbelievable, and worse was hiding it from Leah. "Okay, the truth is, they think that someone we know might be… the diamond smuggler." She held up her hand to Leah. "I know, I know, our crew is like family, it's just that they linked a bunch of Damu's messages to a particular person to dates when I had gigs and, well, they're stalking Damu."

"They think he's involved?"

"I don't know. Sometimes he emails me when he's going to be in town. Which, yes, I realize is fairly often. But he never comes to my concerts so I don't know why they think he might be here to see me. But he is in Amsterdam so they're suspicious. I can't wait for this nonsense to be over. Only two more days, then we'll be home, and everything will go back to normal and…"

Two days and Brody's job would be over. She'd very effectively put that truth behind her. She'd gotten so accustomed to seeing him every morning with her macchiato, and having him standing in the wings of her concerts, and eating his delicious omelets, and…

Hoping she might someday sing for him again. A song of her choosing.

Oh, good grief, she needed to put that out of her mind, too.

"What's that face?" Leah had stopped with her hand on the door. "I knew it! You *are* in love with him, aren't you?"

Ronie froze. "No. Of course not. I mean, what on earth do we have in common? He's bossy and has to be in charge of everything. And then there's the whole… well, he's bossy. And!" She pointed at Leah. "The most glaring reason of all. He is my *bodyguard*."

"I'll say."

"Stop, he's getting paid to do this, if you remember."

"Right. Paid. Of course." Leah smiled. "Do you really think that a guy who is paid would be humming the swing song?" Leah came toward her. "But it's more than that, Rons. Of course you're in love with him—he's the kind of guy you can actually count on more than yourself. And he gets you. He anticipates your moves, like he's studied you—"

"He's supposed to—he's my bodyguard."

"Get over that! Is a bodyguard supposed to hide all the tabloids so you don't get embarrassed?"

He'd been doing that? Funny, now that she thought about it, no, she hadn't seen a tabloid since the day after Damu's birthday party. When she'd mentioned how she'd hated them to Brody...

"Is he supposed to give you tours around Prague and buy you seafood dinners?" Leah's voice held a spark of mischief.

Okay, so maybe he hadn't exactly been a bodyguard that night...

"I know you, Ronie. He's the kind of guy you've always dreamed about, the one on the white horse that will catch—"

"That's enough, Leah. You know I've never been the type who needs catching. And I'm not going to start now."

"Well, maybe you should."

Ronie took her clothes out of her suitcase and began to fill the bureau. She never liked living out of a suitcase, even if it might be for only a few days.

Two days, actually.

Leah touched Ronie's arm. "You don't always have to be your own rescuer, Ronie. You can let someone else do it."

She closed her eyes. "Why *should* he?"

"Are you serious?"

"Yes. I've done nothing but lie to him, and play games

with him, and betray him, and now I'm going to expect him to save my hide? I don't think it works that way."

"That's exactly how it works, honey. That's what love does. It rescues when it doesn't have to—even when it seems like it shouldn't. Love rescues because it *wants* to."

"But he doesn't love me, Leah." Her voice felt so very small.

Leah pulled her into a hug. "I very much disagree with you. But frankly, that's not the problem."

"It's not?"

"No," she said, breaking their hug. "The thing holding you back from Brody isn't his love for you, or even your love for him. It's the fact that you can't love yourself. It's your own feelings of unworthiness that are keeping you from love. You despise yourself for letting your sister, and your mother, and your father—and yourself—down."

Her eyes burned and she turned away. "It wasn't my fault my sister died."

Leah caught her arm. "Keep telling yourself that. Because I'm hoping someday you believe it. But until you do, you could try forgiving yourself. Or at least reach out and let someone help you do it."

She went over to the bedside stand and opened the drawer. "Oh, God bless those Gideons." She picked up the Bible and tossed it onto the bed. "If you need proof, try Romans 5:8. It's a great reminder that even when we didn't know we needed or even wanted forgiveness, God did. It's not about deserving it. It's about God wanting to love you. You're only unforgivable in your own eyes, Miss Vonya."

Ronie picked up the Bible, and ran her thumb over the gold-embossed word. She hadn't been in a church since Savannah's death. Because, yes, how did you face God when you knew you'd failed?

"You might want to consider that God has forgiven you. What gives *you* the right to not forgive you?"

The door clicked shut as Ronie sat down and paged open to the index.

"Our smuggler's actions make perfect sense. It's not hard to mix in contraband diamonds among the official ones."

Chet sat in the living room of his suite, reports spread over the glass-topped table, his computer open. The radio squawked an update now and again from Luke and Vicktor, who had found Damu last night and now parked outside his hotel.

"You think Damu tracked her down, maybe tried to shoot her for taking his computer? But how would he know about the meeting? I still can't get past the idea that this Bishop guy is mixed up in this," Brody said.

"He could be. Or it could be the smuggler—someone who thinks that Ronie is on to him. Or her. Maybe the person knows about Bishop's plan, and they're trying to cut off the source."

Brody paced in front of the table. "We're missing something. The whole operation just feels messy. I want to be there, camped outside his hotel."

"And you want to be *here,* camped outside Ronie's room, too. Trust your team, Wick. That's what we're here for." He made a face. "I learned that in Georgia, when you guys pulled me out of Akif's camp."

Brody looked at Chet, thinking of how Chet had been forced to leave the daughter he'd only just met behind, in Akif's camp. That had to have taken a good-size chunk out of his chest, yet here he was, living, breathing, happily married.

How did a person get there? How did he go from bleeding out on the inside to being patched up and able to reach out and embrace the good things, healing things?

Like...Ronie.

Just being around her, even briefly, felt like something healing and whole inside Brody. Like, for a little while, he could glimpse that power that allowed Chet to sit on the sofa, drinking coffee, letting the sunlight pour into the room.

"Sit down, Wick. You're making me seasick."

Brody squeezed his bulk into a chair. He leaned back. Rubbed his hands on the arms of the chair. Breathed out. Leaned forward. Folded his hands.

"Okay, what?"

"It's just...there are too many unknowns. We're not any closer to figuring out who took a shot at her, and she has another show tonight, and I feel...naked. What if our guy tries something while she's onstage? I can't be beside her there."

A smile crept up Chet's face. "That I'd like to see."

"It's not funny."

"Listen, the crowd will go through a security check as they enter the club. We'll be all over the auditorium, and you'll be ten feet away. She'll be fine."

Brody rubbed his eyes. His head had started to throb, right in the back.

"Wick, there was a reason I wanted you to take R & R. And it had nothing to do with me being out of the office for a month. It had everything to do with the fact that you haven't shaken off what happened in Darfur. You can't forgive yourself for your mistake with Shelby, and for shooting those kids."

Brody winced. He couldn't look at Chet. "I don't want to talk about that."

"I don't care. It's starting to affect your job. You're like a caged lion and it's going to make you sloppy."

"I know. I'm sorry. I'll do better."

"I don't need you to do *better*, Wick. Good grief, if anyone can do this job, it's you. I need you to stop over-thinking this. You have great instincts—use them."

"I can't trust my instincts. I…I feel like I can't trust anything anymore." He hadn't meant to reveal quite that much, but Chet, perhaps, understood him better than anyone. Chet knew what it felt like to make a mistake, to watch someone you love get hurt.

He'd watched the first woman he ever loved be beaten to death right before his eyes. Or, at least, he thought she had died. Try living with that for a couple decades. "How did you get over losing Carissa? Didn't it take you apart inside?"

Chet's face flickered. He swallowed. "Still does, sometimes. But it's then I realize how much in need of a Savior I am. Because I can either let my mistakes consume me, or I can let them bring me to my knees and ask for help."

"I have no idea what you're talking about."

"That's the problem, Wick. See, you always see your-self—I know this about you, because I was the same way—as the guy who can get it done. The oldest of eight—"

"Nine."

"—nine children, the head of your Green Beret unit, the guy who everyone else leans on. You're the go-to man. Somewhere deep inside, you figure that probably you and God are a good team. Equal. You do your part, He does His."

"Isn't that how it works?"

"That's how everyone *thinks* it works—and that's why you have so many people walking around afraid to talk to God. Because, like me, like you, they've blown it. They've dropped their part of the bargain."

Brody stared at his hands.

"But you're not supposed to bring anything to God, Wick. He can't work in your life if you think you can do the job just as well as He can. We have to get to that realization that we have nothing that God needs. Matthew 5:3 says, 'Blessed are the poor in spirit.' In one of my translations, it says, 'Blessed are those who realize their need for Him, or depend only on Him.' It means the paupers in this life, who realize they have nothing to offer God. *Theirs* is the kingdom of heaven. God wants to be your savior, Wick. Just like you're Ronie's."

"I'm not her savior."

"Really? You have her back, you protect her, you guide her in the right places, you rescue her. Just like God does for you. You're not her heavenly savior, but you are the one God appointed to watch over her right now, on earth, for this time."

"And I would do anything to keep her safe."

"Even though she's driven you crazy and pushed you away and lied to you and made a few huge mistakes."

Yes. He wanted to throttle her, too. Or just take her in his arms, hold her tight so the world couldn't hurt her.

"Because you love her."

His head came up and he met Chet's dark gaze. "I don't—"

Chet held up his hand. "Don't even try. I see the way you look at her, the way she fascinates you. She smiles at you and suddenly you're grinning, too. And when this is all over, believe me, we're going to have a conversation about what you plan to do about that. But you know, that's exactly what God does when you let Him be your bodyguard. He *wants* to rescue us. Close protection—with God it takes on a whole new meaning."

Brody's cell phone vibrated in his jeans pocket. He pulled it out. "Ronie's ready to go."

"Why do you think God gave you this assignment? For Ronie's good? Probably. For yours? Definitely. Don't waste it, Wick. Let God watch your back while you watch Ronie's."

Brody tightened his hold on his cell phone as Artyom's voice came over the radio.

"Hey, guys, we just got lucky. I was able to get into Damu's server and set up an alert if he sent another email to our guy. One just came through—he's meeting him now, at the Diamond Exchange, just as you predicted."

Brody stood up. "I can't wait to get my hands on this guy."

"Oh, no, dude. You're on the job." Chet closed his laptop and picked up the radio. "You stay put and let us handle this."

"No way. He nearly killed her. I'm going."

Chet came around the table. "That's precisely why you're staying here. Trust your team, Wick. We'll get him."

FOURTEEN

"Isn't this the most beautiful venue for a concert?" The afternoon sun came through the stained-glass windows above the stage, spotlighting the red carpet below with a messy splotch of colors. Ronie stood in the middle of it, in red and gold light, letting her messenger bag fall to the ground, lifting her arms. "I fell in love with it three years ago, and I don't care that it holds only a limited number—I won't play any other place but the Paradiso. Can you imagine anything more perfect than playing in an old church?"

"It's a little scary from the outside. Dark and melodramatic. And it smells old. Musty, even."

"It's all about presentation, Brody. You should know that by now." She winked at him.

Okay, she'd been acting strange ever since he'd picked her up at her suite.

She hopped up on the stage. "We had to modify the act to fit the venue, but you'll be glad to know we were able to rig up pulleys for the swing song."

"Thrilled beyond words." He followed her onstage and turned out to look at the dance floor. "Are you sure this is the place I approved? Because I remember thinking the crowd could definitely get too close to you here."

She made a face. "Actually, you did turn it down, but Tommy and I chatted and well, okay, at the time, it felt like you were overreacting. Sorry."

Sorry. Sorry was some killer getting on one of those balconies with a gun. "No stage-diving, okay?"

She made another face, picked up her bag and disappeared down the back stairs of the stage.

"Hey, not so fast." He caught up with her, following her down the hall to her dressing room. Her costumes hung on a rack in the hallway.

"The rooms are so quaint, I have to leave the costumes out here."

"*Small* is the word you're looking for." He stopped her before she went in and scanned the room. A mirror, a dressing table already prestocked with her makeup and wigs, as well as a sofa and a dressing screen. "Classy."

"It has character." She plunked her bag onto the table. "Okay, what gives? You've been unusually crabby since we left the hotel."

"No, I haven't." He sat on the sofa, glancing at his watch. Over an hour and not a word.

She shook her head, started unloading her bag, and glanced up at him in the mirror. "Go find a stalker or something."

He narrowed his eyes at her and strode out to the hallway.

Inside her room, she hummed. He heard Chet's words in his head. *You love her...I see the way you look at her, the way she fascinates you. She smiles at you and suddenly you're grinning, too.*

So? Maybe he enjoyed her friendship. She did make him laugh.

And, okay, he would miss her. More than a little. Maybe he'd try to make one of her concerts next time she came to Europe.

He needed a drink of water. Probably she did, too. He poked his head into the dressing room.

She'd applied her fake eyelashes, and for a moment, her eyes seemed so big, so… Man, he needed that drink of water. "Don't open this door until I come back."

"Yes, Oh Protective One." She smirked at him.

He shut the door. On his way to the bar in the back of the church, he radioed in for a status update. No one answered.

He scored some bottled water and returned to the dressing room. He knocked on the door.

"Is that the special code?"

"Funny." But the door opened.

He stood there, his throat parched. "Wow."

"You like it? We're mixing things up for this show."

She wore an indigo-blue sequined dress with a high neck and a cutout at the throat. It slid over her like water. Long gloves added drama that put him right back in the basement tavern, singing the blues. To his surprise, she hadn't added a wig; just her beautiful short brown hair that on her looked downright…

"Close your mouth, Brody. It's just for the opening number."

Right. He opened the water bottle and took a drink. "Uh…" He choked, coughed. "Sorry, I…" Okay. Now he wanted to just shut the door and start over.

"Okay there, pal?"

"Yes, fine. Are there any more changes I should know about?"

"Maybe. I have a new song at the end, instead of the Cha Cha number." She winked at him.

"Listen, I don't know if I can take any more surprises on this trip."

She stepped back, her smile gone. "I'm sorry."

He looked at his watch again. Nearly two hours.

"Brody, what is going on?" She grabbed his lapel, dragged him into the room, pushed the door shut. "You are freaking me out."

He shook his head and ran his hand down his face. When he looked up, she still stood there, hands on her hips.

"I'm not moving until you tell me."

Fine. "Chet and the guys are tracking Damu. He's supposed to be meeting with the smuggler right now. But I haven't heard anything."

"You went after the smuggler and you didn't tell me?"

"Keep your voice down."

"Well, let's go!" And she actually hiked up that pretty dress, as if she might take off in a run.

"You're not going anywhere."

"Listen, I might be able to identify him, did you think of that? You even said that my concert dates had some connection to these handoffs. What if it's someone I know? I should be there."

He actually laughed. She pursed her lips in fury. He schooled his voice. "You know, Ronie, you can't be in charge of everything. You might want to let someone else do something. Like their, I don't know, job?"

He knew her well enough to keep his hand ready for a block.

But instead of anger welling in those beautiful eyes, she actually took a breath and nodded.

"You're right."

He was...*right?* "What?"

"You're right. I can't be in charge of everything. I have to let you do your job. Let you protect me."

"You do?"

She smiled, and then reached out and patted his chest. "Yes. I do. You have everything under control."

No, really, he didn't. He caught her hand before she could feel the thundering of his heart.

"Who are you?"

She laughed, and as usual, it grabbed his breath right out of his chest, clearing his thoughts of everything but her.

"It's still me. It's just the me who is trying to forgive herself and move on. Stop trying so hard to do everything. I'm trying to just let the real Ronie out, and be okay with that."

He never thought it was possible to really want to jump up and sing, but in his head he saw himself leaping to his feet, pulling her into his arms and kissing her right behind her ear, where her neck slid into that collar.

He blinked at her. He wanted to do *what?* "Oh. Uh."

"Are you okay, Brody? You look ill."

"I'm fine. I'm..." But the feeling wouldn't die. "I'm going to...check on...something." He stood, and she stepped away.

"Brody, come in." Chet's voice came through his earpiece.

He met her eyes. "I'm listening."

"He was a no-show. Damu's back at his hotel. We're staying on him, but just so you know, he's still out there. Look alive."

"Confirmed. Keep me updated."

"What is it?" She touched his arm, and he pulled away as if her hand might be a burning coal.

"Sorry. I just…" What? He stared at her, overpowered with the urge to sweep her into his arms and run.

Now she looked hurt. "Did I say something? What's the matter?"

Where did he start? "Yes, something's the matter. We need to cancel the concert."

"What?" She shook her head. "No. Of course not."

"Whoever tried to kill you is still out there. My team didn't get him. And we still have no idea who we are looking for. I can't protect you when I have no idea who—or what—I'm protecting you from."

"Shh." She stepped up to him and put a finger to his lips. "Of course you can."

What if he couldn't? What if she got killed on his watch? He clenched his teeth against the truth but she must have seen it in his eyes because she took his face in her hands. "It's going to be okay. I trust you, Brody."

And then, sweetly, gently, she kissed him. He didn't even know how to respond, just let the taste of her, the smell of her, fill him, calm him.

Protect them both.

Ronie could hear the crowd in this venue better than any other. She stared into the mirror, liking the smoky look that went with this dress. Just wait until Brody heard her newest number. Just her and the mike.

She'd made him smile once before. She could probably do it again.

He hadn't exactly kissed her back in the dressing room. He must have been afraid, right? During her sound check he'd prowled the stage, behind her, before her, like he was caged inside his own world. She'd tried talking to him and he'd nearly bitten her head off.

As if…

No. Suddenly, she saw herself throwing herself into his arms. And him politely pushing her away. Not quite as bad as the moment in Prague, as if she might be diseased, but still…

The truth hit her like a slap. She'd trapped the poor man and, always the gentleman, he didn't want to hurt her feelings. He didn't love her—he was her bodyguard, for crying out loud. Had she been living in her own dream world? Vonya had infected her head.

What a fool she'd become.

She stood and fitted the white wig on her head, adding some indigo-blue glitter around her eyes.

Yes. Better. She'd still sing the blues, but she could keep it from getting personal.

Her eyes filled.

No. She didn't have time to grieve, to cry over her failures.

But what was wrong with her that even after she'd shown him the true Ronie, even after she'd found this pretty dress, even after she'd declared her trust for him, that still he didn't like her?

It wasn't enough to be Ronie. Plain old, unremarkable, insufficient Ronie.

But God demonstrated His own love for us in this… while we were yet sinners, Christ died for us.

She let that verse, the one she read over and over, thrum inside. Like a heartbeat. So maybe, if God liked her, she didn't need Brody to like her, right?

At least, in theory. Because although Brody might lay down his life for her—and oh, please God, don't let it come to that—God already had. He'd already proven it all.

For plain old, unremarkable, insufficient Ronie.

Yes. God liked her. Imagine that.

"Are you okay?" Leah poked her head into the dressing room. "You have about five minutes."

Ronie blinked her eyes and widened them, hoping to dry the tears fast. Leah slipped in, shutting the door behind her. "What's the matter?"

She fanned her eyes. "I'm just so stupid. I practically threw myself at Brody."

Leah didn't look horrified in the least. "About time."

"He doesn't want me. I told you—he doesn't even like me."

Leah shook her head. "He likes you. He just can't show it. Yet. Get though this tour and—"

"And he's gone. He'll put me on a plane tomorrow, and that's it, Leah. He'll walk out of my life. Probably saying good riddance."

"You should have seen him in Prague, when he discovered you were missing. He nearly went out of his mind. He ordered us all to stay at the theater until he came back for us. I think we would have been there all night had Tommy not gone to find Luke and Artyom. Thankfully, they came back to give us the all clear. But by that time, Lyle had fallen asleep on the floor."

Ronie met her eyes in the mirror. "But I saw you come

back right after the show when I was in the square. I saw your light on."

Leah shook her head. "No, we were at the concert hall for a good three hours after the show. Must have been a different room."

"I could have sworn it was your window. Third floor, facing the square?"

"We were on the second floor. Tommy was above us."

"Tommy had that room?" She remembered the light, the figure moving in the window. The light had been on for only a moment or two.

Outside, the band had started to warm up. She took a breath and opened the door. Brody stood in front of her, no expression on his face. He met her eyes a moment before his gaze slid away.

Oh, she hated how she'd dreamed up a future with him. Maybe it hadn't fully crystallized in her mind, but it included walks along the Charles Bridge, and singing to him in his favorite little blues place, and possibly even becoming friends with Gracie and Mae.

Yes, she'd nurtured that impossible daydream a little too long into the night.

She turned, hooking arms with Leah. She didn't need him to love her or even like her. He was just doing his job. Keeping her alive.

Him and his team. Too bad they hadn't caught the smuggler...

"Where was Tommy today?"

"I don't know. He's been working with the sound guys for the past hour or two, though. He forgets we have a stage manager."

Of course he'd been here. Because he wasn't a smuggler.

She stopped at the entrance to the steps. Brody nodded, then moved away to survey the crowd one last time before she took the stage.

One last time. She watched him go, a fortress heading into the black wings.

The crowd had already become deafening.

"Tommy was probably extra-worried," Leah was saying, "because I told him about Brody's concern that someone in our crew might be—"

Ronie whirled to face her. "Leah, you didn't. He knows that Brody is watching everyone?"

"Yeah. He said that Brody was way too suspicious. I agree, I mean, c'mon—"

"Oh, no." Tommy D. He knew her schedule best. In fact, he had full access to her computer and her cell phone so he could transfer files and send reminders if he needed to.

In fact, he'd been the one to set up her cell phone, even devising his own password for her phone, Sigma Alpha Mu, from his fraternity days, plus her birthday: SAM0329.

SAM.

SAM0613. June 13. His birthday.

How could she have missed that?

She could hear her pre-entrance video start up.

Tommy D wouldn't—couldn't—shoot her, right? Where would he get a gun?

Damu. He had security and plenty of weaponry. She'd seen it firsthand. What if Tommy D had read her text message from Bishop? What if Damu knew she'd taken his computer and passed on that information to Tommy?

Then Tommy would have to stop her before she told Bishop what they were doing, where to find him.

"Oh, no. Tommy. You have to tell Brody—"

"Tell him what?"

"That Tommy tried to kill me!"

"Tommy? Why would Tommy want to kill you?"

"Just tell Brody, okay?"

The crowd had begun to chant her name.

Leah turned her toward the curtain separating her from the stage. "Okay, okay. Just get out there onstage."

"I'm not coming off until he finds Tommy. Otherwise he won't go looking for him. I'll be fine with an audience of fans watching and Brody will know exactly where I am."

"What about your swing song?"

"Okay, I'll meet you in the back for that. I'll stay in this costume for the rest."

Leah looked at her with wide eyes.

"Don't worry. I know what to do."

Well, sort of. Her heart hadn't a clue what it might be doing.

But maybe that, too, was up to God.

Please, watch over us all.

She took a breath, pasted on a smile and climbed onto the stage and into the blinding spotlight.

FIFTEEN

That voice. He'd know it anywhere. Brody stood in the wings of the darkened stage, behind a speaker, his eyes on the audience.

Until that voice lifted in the darkness. A cappella, the song started out soft, like a dewdrop sinking into the earth, the melody soaking through the ornate ceilings, through the crowd—through him. He held his breath at her words.

"Eyes that hold me, caring who I might be…"

One single light bathed her, turning her dress into a shimmering indigo flame.

"Arms that catch me or set me free…"

He edged around the front. Her profile was breathtaking, her eyes closed. Her voice became dark chocolate, with hints of cream.

"Maybe I can fly, cross a thousand seas. Yet still he will find me, even in my dreams."

So breakable, like she'd been that first night in the club in D.C. Spikey and tough in Berlin. Sweet butter in the shadows of Prague. The textures of Ronie, each one of them exactly her.

She'd never been hiding. She'd been there all the time.

He pressed his hand to his chest.

"He is my invisible, the only one who sees, reaching…"

"Wick, are you there?" Artyom's voice blared in his ear.

Not now. He ducked back, cupped his hand over his mouth. "What?"

"I just wanted you to know that we got shots of everyone who entered tonight. And Luke and I have eyes on the crowd."

"Perfect. Awesome."

He turned back. The last of her notes, resonant, lay like a blanket over the hushed room, almost as if he were in church. His spirit unhinged from him, made something inside him want to weep.

How was he expected to put her on a plane tomorrow? She'd awakened a dead man.

The light faded and he expected her to rush past him for a costume change, but she stayed onstage, raising her hands to her audience, that smile he knew so well—a real smile—soaking in the applause.

But why hadn't she changed clothes?

Spotlights lit up the stage and her band came to life with her cover song, "Liquid." She took the microphone from the stand, and in that blue dress she became the performer he always knew was behind the mask.

Look into the audience. Stay awake.

This was why he had to put her on a plane. He tore his eyes off her and forced his legs to move him back into the recesses of the stage to watch the crowd. The outlines pressed close, most dancing.

He hadn't a clue whom to suspect.

And the thought nearly compelled him to run onto the stage and sweep her into his arms.

Love—okay, yes, he could admit it, he loved Ronie, loved every crazy side of her—and it terrified him. It threw him off his game.

Why did God give you this assignment?

Chet's words raked through him.

Okay, then, why? So he could make a fool out of himself again? A second chance to fail?

Or a second chance to succeed.

God wants to be your savior, Wick. Just like you're Ronie's.

Maybe God had forgiven him, would even give him a second chance at love with a woman who shared his heart, who wanted to rescue others.

She'd certainly rescued him from the life he'd boxed himself into. From having to hang around every day with the cynical, angry version of himself that had no doubt begun to poison him.

Because of her, he was absolutely going to be on his game. *Please, God, protect her, through me if you have to.*

"Hey, Mr. Brody, did my sister find you?" Lyle edged up behind him. The kid had stayed out of his way for the past week, ever since Brody had barked at him the night Ronie disappeared in Prague. Yes, he felt a little guilty about that. He softened his tone.

"No, Lyle. What's up?"

"She was looking for you—said something about finding Tommy D."

Ronie had finished her number and moved onto a

third. Apparently she planned on staying in that dress. Not a problem with him.

"Where is he?"

"Getting flowers, probably. He always does that the last night of the tour. Then I bring them to her onstage."

Hence, probably the suit and tie on the kid. "That's sweet."

"It's a tradition."

A tradition. The last night of the tour. Meaning, while Vonya was wooing the crowds, Tommy vanished, unaccounted for.

Free to meet with Damu, and hide the diamonds… where?

The light caught her dress, a shimmering spray of light…

Her costumes.

Of course. He might have had them sewn onto her dresses, or even passed off as a prop.

It had been right in front of him the whole time.

"Luke, do you have eyes on Tommy anywhere?"

"Not yet."

"I haven't seen him since before the show," Artyom said.

"I'm checking backstage." He turned to Lyle. "You keep your eyes on her, kid. And if you see Tommy, you come and find me. Pronto."

Lyle nodded.

"Good work."

He grinned.

Brody took off, hearing Ronie's song come to a close.

He ducked into her dressing room. Nothing. He was just turning to leave when she came flying in, nearly plowing right into him.

"I gotta change."

He couldn't move.

"Brody, where's Leah?"

"I don't know. I haven't seen her."

Ronie pushed past him, unzipping her dress.

"Wait, what are you doing?"

"For crying in the sink, Brody, I have a unitard under here. Now help me. I have three minutes—"

He knew he should be averting his eyes, but the zipper wouldn't move and he had to wiggle it down.

Phew, yes, she did have a unitard on. He grabbed the wings and she slipped into them, then the blue high heels. "I'll just have to leave the wig. Did you find Tommy?"

He shook his head. "Why?"

"Because I think he's the one who shot at me."

And then she vanished.

"Wait! Ronie, you can't go onstage!" He took off after her, grabbed her arm just as she reached the curtain.

She turned and gave him a smile. "You'll save me, Boy Scout."

Then she kissed him on the cheek and slipped out onto stage.

You'll save me.

"Find Tommy," he said into his microphone.

He ran around to the stage wing. "Did you see him, Lyle?"

Lyle shook his head. But the kid was clearly looking, and Brody practically wanted to hug him.

"Let's bring up the house lights," he said, but no one responded.

His chest tightened as Ronie sat on the trapeze seat, the fog machine already creating the "clouds" for her song. Her voice lifted, sweet and high.

In a different time and place, he'd liked this song. Like when her feet were safely on the ground.

"I have him on surveillance footage, leaving the Paradiso thirty minutes ago."

"He's going to meet with Damu."

"Wait—there, I see him." Lyle pointed and Brody grabbed his arm, pushing it down.

"Where?"

"Under the Exit sign. Top balcony."

Brody stared at the spot.

A metallic flash.

"Luke, Tommy's got a gun—balcony, right-hand side, go!"

He turned to Lyle, pushing the kid down. "Stay put."

Ronie had begun to swing, way up high above the stage. "Your love gives me—"

A shot cracked the air as Brody vaulted onto the stage. "Ronie, jump! Jump!"

Another shot and her swing pulley exploded.

His heart stopped as she dropped from the ceiling.

Please, God. Please—! He dove and... "Gotcha," he said, cradling her in his arms.

She stared up at him, face white. "You caught me!"

He turned his back to the shooter, scrambling to get her offstage as another shot fired.

Heat blazed across his chest. In his arms, Ronie convulsed. "No!"

He ran down the steps, then set her down amid the screaming. Pandemonium exploded around them. He fell to his knees, searching her costume. Blood spurted out of her chest where the bullet had entered her rib cage.

Her mouth opened. Blood dribbled out.

Another shot. "He's down!" Luke's voice.

So much blood. Brody pulled her to himself, put his mouth to her ear. "Hold on, baby. You're going to be okay." He picked her up. "Make a hole!" he yelled as he jumped off the stage with her and ran toward the entrance. "I need an ambulance, *now!* Ronie, please, stay with me, baby." He kicked open the door to the street, hearing the sirens. "Don't die on me."

Her lips moved and he put his ear next to her mouth.

"You caught me."

He couldn't help it. Brody began to sob.

"Veronica! Come back!"

The sultry breezes of the island caught her long brown hair, tangling it around her face as Veronica ran.

"I want to swing!"

She turned, grinning at Savannah, who emerged from the playhouse, dressed in their mother's discarded party dresses, a black curly wig, a pair of heels spearing into the lawn.

"We're not done playing!"

"I want to swing!" Veronica reached the swing set, crawled onto the leather seat and began pumping her legs.

Savannah stood in the yard, looking pale and thin despite the brilliant sun.

Veronica pumped her golden legs harder, her toes scarred from running barefoot on the flagstone. She gripped the chain, leaned back and let the sun heat her face. "I'm going to fly!"

"You'll just get hurt." Savannah pulled off her wig, her short brown hair not yet grown back. "And then we'll both be in trouble."

"You just don't want Mom to know you're out of bed. But I'm not sick."

Savannah narrowed her eyes and grabbed the other swing. "I can swing higher than you."

"You can't." Veronica leaned forward, pumping harder. Her sister's dress dragged on the ground. "I'm going to jump!"

"Don't!"

Veronica turned at the panic in Savannah's voice, saw her still struggling to pump her swing.

"Watch me, Savannah. Watch me fly!"

"Don't—"

She leaned forward, letting the swing's momentum release her.

She flew. The blue sky caught her and she landed in the soft grass, tumbling to her hands and knees, laughing.

"Did you see me?" She turned back to the swing set.

There was only an empty swing, limp in the wind.

"Veronica, come back, now."

She heard the voice and reached out for the limp swing. "Savannah?"

A hand in hers. Hot. Strong. The yard at Harthaven vanished and she opened her eyes.

White, lots of it. A curtain to her left, and wow, she hurt, all the way to her bones.

"Where—?" Was that her voice?

"You're in the hospital, honey. In Amsterdam."

The senator was here? Dressed in a brown sweater instead of his suit? He looked as if he'd been up all night, pacing. Wait—was it morning?

"How long have I been here?"

"Two days. You had surgery. The bullet collapsed your lung, but thankfully Brody kept you from bleeding out. He practically ran you to the hospital. If it weren't for him—" He blinked and looked away. "Then again, if it weren't for him, maybe you'd never have gone onstage—"

She scrambled for any scrap of memory. Swinging, and Brody yelling, and she looked down and saw him charging across her stage. Then, falling, and pain exploding in her chest…

"He caught me."

Her father ran a thumb under his eye. "That's his job."

He'd caught her. Rescued her. She reached up, wincing at the pinch of an IV and touched her hair. No wig. Just her.

"Where is he?"

"In the hallway, being incorrigible. He had to be pried away from your bed. I told him he's fired, but apparently that hasn't made a dent in his loyalty to you. I finally sent him out for coffee. In fact, the entire security team seems to be pretty dedicated—after they took down Tommy, they found Damu, had him arrested, and they've all been camped out here for two nights."

"Tommy—is he…"

"Alive. Doing better than you. Apparently he's been acting as Damu's smuggler for a couple years now, even before you went to Zimbala. In fact, that's probably why you had such an easy time getting in. Apparently he and Damu met at Harvard—Damu attended one semester. Did you know that?"

She shook her head. "Was Tommy the one who tried to shoot me?"

"Yes, and Damu armed him." He shook his head. "I just can't believe you were involved in this."

"You can't believe I'm involved in a lot of things."

"You're very trusting, you know. Tommy was stealing you blind—I had your accounts checked. He was siphoning away your money. I have no doubt that Damu approached him about helping him transport goods into the country, and they'd worked out your tour with his delivery dates." He ran his thumb over her hand. "Honey, please tell me you didn't do all this because of some obligation to me, or—"

"No, Father. But what are you doing here?"

He frowned. "I should have been here a long time ago, Veronica. A long time ago. I just couldn't bear to…" He bit off his words, turned away.

See her? Have her remind her of the daughter she couldn't save?

"Lose you, too," he finished.

He kissed her forehead. "Do you want to see Brody? I have a feeling this is more than loyalty."

"Really?"

He smiled. "I knew there was something between the two of you. When I saw that newspaper picture of you slapping Wickham outside the club in D.C., I saw something in your eyes—the girl I hadn't seen for years. And I wondered if perhaps Brody Wickham might find the girl that I'd seemed to have lost."

He got up.

"Wait—I'm a mess. I need some makeup, or—"

"You look beautiful. Trust me on this."

"But I need a comb! And a toothbrush!"

He winked at her. "Right."

So maybe she'd never be as beautiful as Savannah, or even Vonya, but at least she wouldn't frighten small children. She finally declared herself as presentable as she could be in a pink hospital gown and unwashed hair.

How unfair could it be that a couple of sleepless nights only made Brody more breathtaking? With his beard growth, his dark, mussed hair, his trademark black T-shirt, a pair of worn jeans—and bloodshot eyes.

He stood at the end of her bed for a long, terrible moment, shaking his head, and she just wanted to reach out to him. To pull him into her arms. But for all his dedication he seemed afraid to touch her. "Oh, Ronie. What would I have done if you had died?" His hands whitened on the bed and he looked down, drew in a breath.

"But I didn't. Because of you. You caught me, and you kept me alive. You saved me, Brody."

"I nearly didn't." He lifted his head, his gaze fierce. "I held you in my arms, and thought—"

"You thought I was going to die, just like Shelby."

"No. Shelby's death took me apart, but yours…well, I would have crawled right into the grave with you." He closed his mouth, his lips a hard line. "You don't understand. I didn't rescue you." He took a breath and finally moved around the bed and took her hand in his. "You rescued me."

"I don't understand."

"I was just half alive when I met you. That night at the club, when I plowed through the crowd and found you huddling under a speaker, something sparked inside me. I would have never guessed it was my heart coming back to life, but being with you—you made me want to be more. Made me want to know you, to discover the real Ronie. And when I did…" He smiled. "It had to be you, baby, who turned my life from blue."

"That's a terrible version."

"Yeah, well, it's better than yours." He leaned over and finally gently, sweetly kissed her. So sweetly, it could steal her already fractured breath from her. He ran his fingers down her face, and seemed to breathe her in even as he pulled away, kissing her forehead.

"So. You like me?"

She wasn't sure where the words came from, and didn't intend for them to be quite so pitiful.

"Yes. I like you. A little." Then he shook his head. "Okay, more than a little. I'm crazy about you." He swallowed, his beautiful eyes suddenly serious. "I love you, Ronie. Every side of you."

He kissed her again, this time with a little more determination.

He tasted fresh, his touch full of grace. She couldn't believe this amazing, breathtaking hero belonged to her.

Yes, oh yes, Brody Wickham had caught her.

She smiled. "I love you, too, Boy Scout. You make me feel safe."

"I do?"

She rolled her eyes. "I don't suppose you're available for my next tour?"

"Wonder Girl, I'm available for your every tour."

He moved away then, something new in his eyes. "And don't you worry about Kafara anymore. I've got the whole thing under control."

Of course he did.

EPILOGUE

"*Stay put.*"

The last words Brody said to Ronie hammered in his mind like a heartbeat as he lay in the brush outside Mubar's training camp, hiding amid the tall grasses under a scrub mopane tree.

In the indigo darkness, under a too-clear midnight sky, the camp lay below, tin roofs painted black, shiny under a half-moon. Around him, the savanna rustled, the smells of dry earth in his nose, crickets buzzing, the occasional screech of a bird, mosquitoes in his eyes. He didn't move.

Bishop's information had better be good, or he'd track the man down again, and this time he wouldn't be civil. Sorry, but the CIA handler's answer of *national security* and *the government's best interests* didn't in the least satisfy Brody's questions. Brody wondered if Bishop ever had any intention of wasting time liberating Kafara or just intended to continue to milk Ronie for more favors.

He'd done the guy the favor of keeping him out of the hospital. In return, of course, for every last scrap of intel about Mubar's camp and Kafara's current location.

"All set, Wick, Artyom. Move in," Chet said in Brody's earpiece. Some ten feet away, Brody could barely make out Artyom's form as the man proceeded toward the camp.

Brody followed his own route, past the two child guards, their AK-47s lying across their laps. They didn't have a prayer of seeing Brody as he slipped past.

He crouched behind a shed—one of the completely enclosed buildings that Brody had no doubt was used for weapons storage—then hit the ground and crawled toward the free-standing shacks.

Two days of surveillance told him that Kafara had a bed near the back—and that Mubar ran a tight, brutal camp, training true killing machines.

He'd had to put a lid on his fury—it had the ability to turn him inside out, or take him apart with the memories.

For Ronie, he'd do this.

For Ronie, he'd sneak into Hades and back, if she asked it.

"Set," Artyom said, and Brody moved toward the structure. He stayed low next to the sleeping bodies, row after row of them, curled on ratty blankets, some with cuts on their pudgy dark faces, others shivering, the chilly savanna air finding their dreams.

Or nightmares.

Someday soon, he'd return with more than just the Stryker team, if he and Ronie had their way. Behind him, Artyom captured the entire thing on video. Perfect for an exposé and, hopefully, international pressure.

And if he happened to start a revolution to overthrow

General Mubar, well, that wouldn't exactly keep Brody up at night.

Kafara, dressed in an oversize army jacket and thread-bare pants, slept as if protecting himself, his body in a fetal position. How many of these kids were high? Too many times he'd seen children being forced to take drugs in order to make them more violent.

He clamped a dirty hand over Kafara's mouth and whispered in the boy's ear, speaking the words he'd memorized in Kafara's language: "Vonya sent me. Say nothing."

The boy's eyes opened. He shook and Brody clamped a hand across his shoulder. "Don't move."

Kafara stilled, probably terrified.

"Vonya sent me," Brody repeated. Please, please let their intel be correct. What if Kafara lay across the room, or in yet another tent, or even buried under the rubble of a charred village?

The boy nodded. Brody had no time for relief. "Follow me. Quiet."

Still, he held the kid a moment longer before he released his hand from his mouth.

Kafara took a breath. Brody held his. Then, Kafara rolled over, got to his knees and looked at Brody. He nodded.

Brody led them out of the shelter, running until they reached the shadows of the storage building. How he'd like to leave a little present—a couple of grenades, per-haps. But their only objective was to rescue Kafara.

"Stop."

The voice could have shouted, could have alerted the

entire camp. But it came out a whisper, and that gave Brody hope even as he turned.

He recognized the boy as one of the three in Ronie's picture. He was dressed in ripped fatigues, a grimy T-shirt.

And holding an AK-47. He leveled it at Brody's chest.

"Chuma." Kafara turned to him, speaking in Zimbalan. Chuma shook his head, his eyes on Brody.

Brody lifted his hands.

"I've got him, Brody," Luke said quietly into Brody's ear. "Give me the word."

"Hold," Brody said softly. He looked at the kid, placing him at about thirteen. "Listen, Chuma, I hope you can understand me…" He took a breath, putting as much compassion into his tone, his eyes, as he could. "Come with us. Right now. Put the gun down and come with us. You don't have to stay."

Chuma stared at him without blinking. Without moving.

Kafara glanced at Brody and spoke again to Chuma in a low tone.

The boy shook his head.

"We're running out of nighttime here, Brody."

"Hold, Luke."

Please, God, I'm trusting You…

He could reach out and grab the gun, turning it on Chuma faster than the kid could even take a breath.

And he could probably even take out a good portion of the camp before getting Kafara to safety.

How, then, would he live beyond that? He stared at Chuma, saw sweat beading on his upper lip, saw the way the weapon shook, ever so slightly in his hand. This kid didn't want to kill him. Not really. He just didn't want a beating for disobeying orders, for being responsible for Kafara's disappearance.

And Brody couldn't live with killing another kid.

Not breaking Chuma's gaze, he lowered himself to his knees and held up his hands. "I mean you no harm. But you can come with me, and wake up a free man. You have a choice, Chuma. Right now."

He could practically taste his pulse.

I trust You, God.

And, strangely, all fear left him. Just the last remnant of something he'd been hanging on to—perhaps fear of himself, even. But as he stared at Chuma, he suddenly felt…free.

"Stand down, Luke," he whispered.

He met Chuma's dark, wide eyes. "Trust me," he said.

Maybe the boy did understand English. Maybe it was Kafara, still pleading with him in Zimbalan, but suddenly something crumpled on Chuma's face. He took a shuddering breath and lowered his gun.

Brody pushed the barrel away from his chest and nodded to Chuma. "Let's go."

Chuma released the weapon into Brody's hands. Then Brody turned and, motioning them to stay down, waited for the all clear from Chet to hustle outside the camp.

He crouched with the boys in the bush. They looked at him, fear on their faces. "Don't worry, boys. You're safe. Welcome to freedom."

"Stay put? Does Brody have any idea what he's asking of me?" Ronie stared out into the jagged outline of the savanna, desperate for any sign of the team.

"Oh, I think so." Mae sat in the door of the helicopter, her curly red hair tied back from her face, blending into the night in her black fatigues. "Be glad he let you come this far, especially with you still recuperating. In fact, you're supposed to be in the chopper."

"I know you're ex-military and all that, but really, don't try anything."

Mae laughed. "Oh, I get it, believe me." She took off her gloves, got down and came to stand beside Ronie. "Don't worry. They'll be here. The Stryker team is a get-it-done bunch of guys."

Ronie ran her hands over her arms. "I hate this. How do you live with the waiting?"

"I just pray. A lot."

Ronie understood the praying part. She had a new appreciation for communication with God since Brody had caught her in Amsterdam. And lying in a hospital bed, counting her blessings, she'd learned a side of "God liked her" that she hadn't exactly thought possible.

But perhaps that was what real love felt like. Not deserved, but a gift. She suddenly realized she was humming.

"What is that you're singing?" Mae asked.

"It's a song I'm working on or, rather, honing. For a new album. *Ronyika Sings the Blues.*" Yes, that had a nice ring to it.

Mae raised an eyebrow. "What happened to Vonya?"

"I think Vonya has had her time."

"I think you'll have an entirely new set of fans."

Hmm. Maybe. It seemed easier in the past three weeks to break free from Vonya a little more every day. After the dramatic finish to her tour in Amsterdam, and her disappearance, all sorts of internet rumors emerged. She especially loved the abducted-by-aliens stories.

Mae lifted her night-vision goggles to her eyes, scanning the terrain. "I think I see them."

It could spook a girl right through to her bones the way the team bled right out of the darkness. Their black outlines sent a thrill through her, especially when she made out the forms of—wait, *two* teenagers?

But she stayed put. Because Brody had asked her to.

He showed his teeth as he cleared the brush. "I brought you someone," he said, and then, emerging from the darkness, she saw a wide-eyed Kafara, thinner maybe, still so handsome, his eyes shiny.

She couldn't move. "Kafara?"

"Miss Vonya? Is that you?" He wore an oversize jacket that nearly swallowed him, but when he grinned, there was the boy she'd fallen in love with.

"Yes, Kafara. It's me. The real me." She reached out and drew him close. "I'm so sorry it took so long."

He clung to her, his body beginning to shake as his breath caught.

"Shh. You're safe now. You're safe."

She pulled away, cradling his face in both hands. "Want to come home with me?"

His smile was slow, as the words seeped into him. Then, he nodded.

She looked past him to his friend, at the confused look on his face. "I recognize you," she said quietly.

"This is Chuma," Brody said. "He…needs a home, too."

"He has one." She took his hand and looked up at Brody. "I don't suppose you can convince Bishop to get him a visa, too?"

Brody nodded, something dangerous in his expression. "Bishop still owes us a few favors."

Mae had already affixed her helmet and was climbing into the cockpit. "Let's go."

Chet climbed in next to Mae. Luke and Artyom helped the boys in and strapped them into the seats.

Ronie touched Brody's arm. "Are you ready for some real R & R now?"

He met her eyes, a slight grin on his face. "Can you promise me peace and quiet?"

She raised up on her toes, her voice low. "Oh, I sincerely doubt it."

He laughed. The sound of it made her want to soar. Then, he reached down and swooped her into his powerful arms, pressing a quick kiss to her mouth.

He turned them toward the chopper. "I think peace and quiet are highly overrated anyway."

"You're right. I can't seem to stay out of trouble. Maybe I should hire a bodyguard."

He settled her inside the chopper, buckled her in and sat beside her as Mae maneuvered it into the air.

"Not necessary," he said, close to her ear. "That job's taken."

* * * * *

Dear Reader,

My family claims that I sound different on the phone, or when I am speaking, than I do in "real" life. They're partly right. When I'm doing a signing or a women's event, I have a way about myself that might not be the same gal you'd see on the other side of the computer, hidden away in my office. We all live "double lives," based on what we want people to see and the things we're trying to prove to ourselves. I took that premise and applied it wildly to Ronnie, aka Vonya, and Brody, who also wants to be seen as capable and not broken. But we're all a little broken, and we hide our failures and mistakes, thinking we need to make up for them to be forgiven and approved. But forgiveness isn't an equation—it's a gift. Only when we accept it can we take off our masks and become the people we are intended to be.

Susan May Warren

QUESTIONS FOR DISCUSSION

1. At the start of the story, Brody finds himself in a place he'd rather not be, doing something he'd rather not do. What is it and how does it turn out for good? Have you ever been in a place you'd rather not be…and had it turn out differently than you had expected?

2. Vonya lives a life much different from her parents—different from their values and lifestyle. Have you had a member of your family or a close friend who has chosen a much different life than your family culture? How has that affected your relationships? Does that person choose to put on a mask when they are with their family?

3. What is Veronica's motivation for going on tour overseas (besides her career)? Are there any global causes that would make you behave/do something out of your comfort zone to help?

4. Brody at first believes the "mask" Vonya wears. When is the first time he sees her as someone different? Have you ever made a first impression about someone only to have it shattered later? When and how?

5. The tour visits a number of European locations. Have you ever been to Europe, or even to one of Vonya's concert locales (Berlin, Prague and Amsterdam)? What was your favorite location and why?

6. Vonya has a recurring nightmare about what she fears. Have you ever had a recurring nightmare? Was it something you feared, or something from your past? (Or neither?)

7. What is Veronica's deep secret that she just can't forgive herself for? How does that keep her from being able to accept Brody's love? Do you think our past contributes to our ability to love—and to let others love us? How?

8. What is Brody's deep secret? Have you ever had to do something you disagreed with, that haunted you afterward?

9. If you could be a rock star or a musician…what would you be like?

10. Chet suggests that God had assigned Brody to protect Veronica not only for her good but his, also. Why? Has God ever given you an assignment that seemed over your head, or even useless, to surprise you with a lesson? What lesson was it?

Love Inspired®
SUSPENSE

TITLES AVAILABLE NEXT MONTH
Available April 12, 2011

REQUEST YOUR FREE BOOKS!

2 FREE RIVETING INSPIRATIONAL NOVELS
PLUS 2 FREE MYSTERY GIFTS

Love Inspired®
SUSPENSE

YES! Please send me 2 FREE Love Inspired® Suspense novels and my 2 FREE mystery gifts (gifts are worth about $10). After receiving them, if I don't wish to receive any more books, I can return the shipping statement marked "cancel". If I don't cancel, I will receive 4 brand-new novels every month and be billed just $4.24 per book in the U.S. or $4.74 per book in Canada. That's a saving of at least 23% off the cover price. It's quite a bargain! Shipping and handling is just 50¢ per book in the U.S. and 75¢ per book in Canada.* I understand that accepting the 2 free books and gifts places me under no obligation to buy anything. I can always return a shipment and cancel at any time. Even if I never buy another book, the two free books and gifts are mine to keep forever.

123/323 IDN FDCT

Name _____ (PLEASE PRINT) _____

Address _____ Apt. # _____

City _____ State/Prov. _____ Zip/Postal Code _____

Signature (if under 18, a parent or guardian must sign)

Mail to the **Reader Service:**
IN U.S.A.: P.O. Box 1867, Buffalo, NY 14240-1867
IN CANADA: P.O. Box 609, Fort Erie, Ontario L2A 5X3

Not valid for current subscribers to Love Inspired Suspense books.

**Are you a subscriber to Love Inspired Suspense
and want to receive the larger-print edition?
Call 1-800-873-8635 or visit www.ReaderService.com.**

* Terms and prices subject to change without notice. Prices do not include applicable taxes. Sales tax applicable in N.Y. Canadian residents will be charged applicable taxes. Offer not valid in Quebec. This offer is limited to one order per household. All orders subject to credit approval. Credit or debit balances in a customer's account(s) may be offset by any other outstanding balance owed by or to the customer. Please allow 4 to 6 weeks for delivery. Offer available while quantities last.

Your Privacy—The Reader Service is committed to protecting your privacy. Our Privacy Policy is available online at www.ReaderService.com or upon request from the Reader Service.

We make a portion of our mailing list available to reputable third parties that offer products we believe may interest you. If you prefer that we not exchange your name with third parties, or if you wish to clarify or modify your communication preferences, please visit us at www.ReaderService.com/consumerschoice or write to us at Reader Service Preference Service, P.O. Box 9062, Buffalo, NY 14269. Include your complete name and address.

LISUS11